This book is dedicated to my Composition teacher, Mrs. Agy, due to her insight about my writing talent. Also, to my friends and co-editors Michael Carsten and Alesia Carsten who always support my efforts in whatever I choose to do!

Last but never least my loving and supportive husband Miguel!

1

Tree of Many Lives:

Slave to Abuse

By Kellie England

Tree of Many Lives: Slave to Abuse
Copywrite ©   2007 by Kellie England
All rights reserved. Printed in the United States of America. No part of this book may be used or reproduced in any manor whatsoever without written permission except in the case of reprints in the context of reviews. For information, inquire at www.Lulu.com ID:1032045.

ISBN: 978-0-6151-5747-4

Book design by Michael Carsten and Thomas England

Book Cover Art "Tree Kingdom Palace" Copywrite © 2007 deviantART Inc.

Chapters

Prologue

This day would be better, it would be different. He said he loved her and would never hurt her again. She had heard all the same promises day after day, throughout the entire five years of her marriage to him that she had suffered through, but as of yet, not one single promise had been kept. Her slumped shoulders, unkempt hair, drawn facial expressions, and severely baggy clothing showed how very much her husband did not love her. They gave away all the lies she had told to the many doctors over the years of abuse suffered from him. The hospital staff would just nod their heads in disgust, as if she could honestly do anything to help her situation; after all what did they expect? Did they really think she was capable of giving a full testimony of what happened inside the prison she called her home? It was not even a twinkle in her eye, a thought in her head, because as many times as he had promised never to do the atrocities to her that he preformed on her daily; twice as many times he had also told her he would kill her if she ever told anyone about them.

Tamaria Jackson was once a very beautiful woman. In her youth her skin had shown smooth and flawless; the color of caramel. Her eyes were bright and inquisitive always looking deeply into the eyes of the person whose attention she was capturing. Tamaria had laughed and giggled at the smallest things; finding joy in each day that she was graced with. She knew that having something to smile about was what made life worth living; after all she lived with a controlling and mean natured father that never let her out of his sight. Tamaria tried to make the best of her life by enjoying the moments she had with friends and other family members. She could not ever be found outside of her home looking anything less than her best, even though many times she found herself in trouble with her father for looking like a slut; she believed that first impressions lasted a lifetime and bad impressions an eternity. Everyone that came in contact with Tamaria found her captivating, which may have been her biggest fault; her own father acted as if she should be sold to the highest bidder. When Darien had walked into her life she thought she had found a loop hole towards her own happiness; her father was pleased to get her off of his shoulders once he received a large sum of money from Darien. She had thought, at the time, that Darien must really

8

love her to pay her Daddy off in order to marry her, but now Tamaria felt alone and vulnerable every minute of every hour each day she survived.

Living was the more painful of the choices she had in life, the cowardice she felt kept her from ending her life. She waited for her husband to take things to far, and end her misery once and for all. Perhaps fate would hear her prayers for death and step into the picture to help her out, perhaps fate could show her the path to redemption; maybe she would be given the answers to the same questions she cried into her pillow every night until she fell to sleep. Why me God, what did I ever do to deserve this, what lessons can I possibly learn from anything that is happening to me?

Chapter One
The Beginning

Oh dear God, he would be home soon and she was late! How was she ever going to get his supper on the table in time? He would kill her for having gone out for coffee with her sister; he hated it when she talked to anyone else but him. Darien was so possessive and controlling. She had suffered the consequences many times before for going outside of his rules to visit her sister, why had she done this to herself again, she kept thinking. I know better than to aggravate him, what was wrong with my head this morning.

The steaks were still frozen, but she could de-thaw them in the microwave for a few minutes, hopefully they would be ready to cook quickly. She grabbed some potatoes and a sharp knife to cut them with, and then headed to the cutting board. Very quickly and with great skill she sliced the potatoes thinly into a frying pan and threw in a large chunk of butter and some garlic. She reached over the cookie jar and grabbed the salt and pepper sprinkling them both over the pan; then deftly set the pan back onto the stove top to cook. With no thought to her clothing she grabbed the steaks out of the microwave when the bell rung to announce the finished product, it was as she pulled them out quickly that the blood flew across her sweater in tiny splattered ovals. Tamaria let out a yelp of fear realizing the punishment she would receive for dirtying the top; it was Darien's favorite one that she wore. She almost sat down and wept with frustration for her own situation, but decided to try to at least get Darien's supper done before he got home. Maybe that would ease his anger at her for all the other stupid things she had done that day, doubt lingered in the back of her mind.

As Tamaria reached to grab a spatula to flip over the steak and potatoes, she heard the car pull in the driveway. She scrambled to get the broccoli in a pan and cooking before Darien walked through the door; making it with only three seconds to spare. As Darien came into the house he noticed that he could not smell his supper, he wondered what Tamaria had cooked for him and why he couldn't smell it. All he could think of was a big juicy hamburger and some fries, she damn well better have a hamburger waiting for him. He had been hungry all day and hadn't stopped long enough

11

in between clients to get some lunch. He had been sure Tamaria was at home planning a lovely grilled dinner for him, and if she hadn't she'd be very sorry.

"Tamaria, where are you and what's for supper?" he growled as he walked into the dining room and noticed that there was no food on his table.

"I'm right here Darien," she said as she walked into the room from the kitchen, "I hope you had a wonderful day at work," she finished hoping to get his mind of the dining room tables missing dinner.

"It was a pretty good day until now!" he yelled at her. "I was so swamped with clients that wanted new cars that I didn't have any time to eat lunch, so I hope dinner is ready."

"Well you must be pretty happy with the money that you made, so why are you so upset?"

"Don't play dumb with me woman, why isn't my supper on this damn table?"

"Oh, don't worry Darien, it's coming right now. I'll go get it. Please don't get yourself all worked up, I promise you'll love what I made. I'm sorry you had to miss your lunch. I should have been more prepared, but I wasn't feeling very well this afternoon," she said lacking the confidence in her own words, but hoping he believed her.

"For your sake I hope I love the meal you made! What was wrong with you this afternoon? Another headache? You seem to get enough of them in the evenings before bed. I'm really getting tired of you pissing me off everyday when I get home from work. What possesses you to aggravate me?" he replied as if he had been treated very badly for as long as he could remember.

Tamaria quickly placed the under cooked food on his plate and prayed that he was too hungry to notice. She walked through the doorway into the dining room and instantly felt the change in him. His shoulders had stiffened, his lips were curled back in an almost maniacal expression, and the nostrils of his nose were flared out as far as they could humanly go. She began to shake and walk a little slower, all the while watching for any signs that he was about to strike out at her. As she set the plate down in front of him, he reached out and grasped her wrist in a death hold that stopped the circulation to her fingers, making them numb and painful. She winced in pain, but made no sound, she had learned to take his abuse quietly or she would receive a lot more.

Through gritted teeth he asked, "Where were you today that kept you so busy for so long of a time, that you couldn't even cook your husband a proper dinner?"

Afraid to answer, she lied carefully, 'I wasn't gone long, really it was so quick, and I just needed to run to the store for the potatoes. I thought you would like to have some with your steak, I know how much you like the way I cook them. I'm sorry the dinner is a little under cooked, I wasn't feeling well this afternoon and when I sat down to stop the room from spinning I fell asleep on the sofa. Please forgive me, I'll go cook all of this till it's done, just give me a few minutes. It'll only take a few I promise," she pleaded.

He flared at her like a lit piece of dynamite and she saw the hate leaking into his face as he listened to her nonsense. She knew he did not believe her and wanted to run away from him, but he had a hold of her and she couldn't. "So you needed potatoes, huh, well what do you say you go get the receipt for the potatoes? I would be very interested in seeing what the going rate for potatoes is these days." "Oh I can't do that, I put the bag and the receipt in the garbage. It would be dirty, I'm not even sure if I didn't accidentally drop it down the disposal" she said as she looked down at her feet. "You lying bitch, what do you take me for? A stupid ass? Well I have had all I can take of your aggravation; it's time you learned a lesson. Why must you force me to teach you how to behave properly? I don't enjoy these times, I hope you know that," he said with excitement in his voice.

"No, oh please no, I promise I'll fix the dinner and make it good. I'll never leave the house again without your permission, please don't hurt me again," she cried pitifully.

Damien dragged Tamaria across the dining room as he shut each one of the blinds, then into the living room to do the same. All the while Darien was kicking her here and there to get his aggressions out. As he closed the last blind in the lower part of the house he turned and lashed out at her before she could dodge the punch. The only sound that she heard was that of her own neck and jaw snapping back. She saw stars, slowly the room dimmed to black and she fell backward into the fireplace slamming her head into the brick. Blood began to flow so quickly that a puddle soon formed. She felt the warmth of her own blood as it trickled down her head onto the floor underneath her. She slowly slipped into unconsciousness. Damien glared down at his wife with loathing. "Get up you stupid cunt, I said get up," he yelled at her as he kicked her in the ribs. When she didn't make a move or a sound he stepped over her body bending down to grab her hair; he shook her lifeless body with the strength of three men splattering blood up and down the glass front of the fireplace cover. When he realized she was out cold and that she refused to come to, he let out a loud curse and kicked her for not waking up. He looked down once again and decided to leave her where she was, he wasn't carrying her upstairs; she deserved to sleep on the floor for her stupidity and lies. He turned and headed for the door deciding to go out and get the hamburger he had been craving all afternoon after all, as far as his wife was concerned, she could lay there and bleed to death he didn't really care. No one had ever given a damn about him when he was hurting, so why should he feel bad for her?   Tamaria slowly came to, she tried to move her head, but the searing pain that shot through her neck and up into her scalp stopped her cold. Where was she? What happened? She tried to remember how she had gotten hurt, but couldn't seem to gather her thoughts together enough to regain the memory. She reached up and gingerly touched the top of her head, the sticky substance in her hair was still wet; she realized it was her own blood. She tried to sit up but didn't have enough strength to pull herself to a sitting position; it was then that she knew she was hurt badly and needed to go to a hospital. She slowly rolled over and put her right arm in front of her, moving in a semi-army crawl across the floor; all the while leaving a trail of blood behind her as she went. She was about four feet from the portable phone on the lamp stand, when it began to ring; the sound reverberated through her skull like a bomb going off in a tin can. The noise caused so much pain in her head that she almost passed out. She closed her eyes and focused on staying conscious, knowing she needed to get to that phone and ask whoever was on the other end for help. Taking a deep breath she gathered up just enough strength to launch herself towards the lamp stand, knocking the phone off of its base. She grabbed it and pushed the on button just as her sister was about to hang up, "Hello, hello is anyone there," she could hear her sister yelling.

"Help me, Natillie, I'm hurt," was all she could get out before she slipped into sweet darkness once again.

"Tamaria, is that you? Tamaria please answer me!" her sister screamed. "If you can hear me Tamaria, I'm coming over, I'll be there soon!" Natillie yelled as she slammed the phone down and ran out her door to go help her sister.

It was the longest drive Natillie had ever taken in her life, she was so scared that Damien had finally did it, that he had killed her sister. All the way across town to her sister's house in the outskirts of Savannah she swore to herself that if she found her sister dead, she would hunt that son of a bitch

17

down and kill him herself. God, why wouldn't Tamaria just leave the jerk? She deserved so much better. She turned down Miracle Avenue, and sped straight to the driveway of her sister's house. Natillie glanced at the mailbox that sat in front of her sister's house, the numbers that were attached to its side read 666; Natillie had told Tamaria the house was cursed with an address like that. Natillie hit the brakes and jumped out of her car without ever turning her engine off; she ran to the front of the house and pushed the door open; thank God Darien was so mindless as to leave it unlocked. She frantically looked in the kitchen, then the dining room, and at last the living room, before she saw Tamaria lying face down on the floor with a trail of blood leading to the puddle that was under her head. Natillie screamed and ran to her sister, "What has he done to you? Oh dear God, please be okay, please, please be okay," she mumbled. She looked to the side of her sister and saw the portable phone lying next to her; it was still on and making the horrible noise of a phone left off of the hook for too long. As Natillie picked the phone up she pressed the button to turn it off, then back on and dialed 911.

The ambulance was there in fifteen minutes, but to Natillie it seemed like an eternity. Her sister had never regained consciousness while she sat waiting for the emergency vehicle to arrive, holding her sister's bloody upper body in her lap. Nor did Tamaria come to on the ride to the hospital. The EMT's kept asking Natillie what had happened, how her sister had been injured; all Natillie could tell them was that she had only heard her sister's pleas for help over the phone, nothing else. She knew Darien had something to do with this, but right now her sister's survival was more important than revenge. Later, however, would be a very different story; Natillie would find a way to teach Darien a very rough and painful lesson.

Chapter 2

Dr. Chasm Liteseeker and the Trauma Room

Another abuse victim, God how she hated dealing with these women and there ignorance, when would women that were in abusive relationships stand up for themselves and stop the abuse. How much could a woman take before they realized they needed to get out of a dangerous situation? Dr. Chasm Liteseeker had spent most of her fifteen year medical career trying to help these women, but in the last two years she had decided enough was enough; she would force them to take a closer look at reality one way or another.

Chasm wasn't your normal doctor, for that matter she wasn't really a normal human being. She was a forty-five year old woman, that didn't look a day over thirty. Somehow time had stood still for her. Her face bore not one single wrinkle, mark, or even a slight blemish; she had a complexion that resembled fresh peaches and cream, her eyes were an unusual shade of blue and purple mixed together to make periwinkle, and they were framed in thick, long golden lashes that swept her cheeks when she blinked. The luxurious hair framing her heart shaped face was of the same golden shade as her lashes, but just a touch lighter and brighter. Her lips were dark pink and smooth as satin, making every man want to experience there touch. Chasm was a very special lady indeed; she was magical in every sense of the word.

When Chasm was just a small girl she had discovered that she was different than the other girls that she played with. She had dreams, lots of them, but that wasn't what made her different or special, it was the fact that those dreams came true within a week of her having them. She would view the future at night in her sleep and in the morning wait to see when it would happen. Over time she began to use it to her advantage and avoid things that were negative or trouble for her, but just about when she began to gain a grasp on her insight, other odd occurrences began to happen to and around her. She would be thinking of things she wanted to do or places she wanted to go and out of the blue her mother would come into the room and ask her why she wanted to do those things and go to those places. She was sending her thoughts into other peoples' minds. She soon realized that she could communicate with others without ever opening her mouth, most of the time they never noticed that she hadn't spoken to them, but when they did; they just put it off to coincidence. As she grew into a young woman she felt her strength getting more and more powerful; her energies were phenomenal. She decided to go into the field of medicine, and put her powers to good use helping others. With every passing year she grew stronger and more capable of healing and changing the influences around her. Then about thirteen years into her career, when she was beginning to become disillusioned about abuse patients that she dealt with daily, she discovered an inner space that was so powerful that she could actually project her patients into it. One day while she was treating a young woman that had been into the emergency room five times that week alone, she tried to talk to the patient about leaving her husband behind and seeking a divorce. The woman became irate and insisted that her husband loved her and would never knowingly hurt her, she would never leave him. Chasm became so furious that she began to think of ways to teach this young lady a lesson on the importance of life and the protection of ones own being, as she dreamt up new and more drastic ways to get the young woman's attention and make her see the error in her choices a funny rumble began in the back of her head. She found herself glancing around the hospital partition to see what was making such a loud noise, but nothing was there; so she went back to her day dreaming while stitching up the patient's cheek. Again the rumble began, only this time a shimmering, swirling, vortex started to form just behind Chasm's patient's head. Chasm stared at it and watched the movement and changes that occurred with each new thought she began in her head. She started to get scared and decided she had better ignore this odd movement of her energy, so she turned back to the job at hand, and noticed the young woman had fallen asleep. She gently shook her to wake her up after finishing the stitches, but the woman didn't move. There was no life in the woman, no acknowledgement of Chasm's presence. She checked her vital signs and noticed the pulse was dropping very fast and her breathing was becoming shallow. Chasm ran out of the cubicle and yelled code blue to the nurses around her. Suddenly the ER was a mass of running medical personnel and doctors trying to keep this injured woman alive. When the patient's vitals were stabilized she was taken to the Intensive Care Unit, she had gone into a coma and nothing the hospital's staff had done seemed to bring her out of it. The worst of it was that no one could explain how it had happened or why. Chasm sat down in complete disbelief of what had just occurred she was stunned and confused, but she knew somehow, someway she had created that woman's comatose state. She was becoming dangerous and she didn't know what to do about it.

Over the past two years Chasm had come to call the energy bursts that created the coma vortex for some of her worst female abuse cases, The Tree of Many Lives. When the women who had the fortunate, or perhaps unfortunate, experience of this phenomenon began to come out of their comas, they would describe an enormous mystical tree, with a door that allowed entrance to the tree, as the place they had been during their comatose state. Dr. Liteseeker never knew which patients would find themselves standing at the entrance door of the huge tree due to her energy, but those that did never came out of it the same as they went in. All of the women had benefited from their very similar, yet extremely different experiences. All of the women went to the same tree, and were drawn to enter the same door, but once inside; the tree spoke to each individual telling them where to go in the maze of unending hallways and millions of doors leading off of them. Each woman had to enter their own door to find the answers to the many questions their lives had created for them, and The Tree of Many Lives was the portal through which they experienced a new existence that would help them to find those answers. It seemed that the tree allowed them the time to make important choices so they could learn new lessons and benefit from their current lives, no matter the severity of their situations. A few women never returned from the tree, having chosen the alter-life as their new current life and lesson. The tree was a tool to push the victims into moving forward. It was a place where a person could find permanent anonymity.

On this particular day Dr. Liteseeker was staring down at the face of Tamaria Jackson and wondering just how many times she had treated this very same woman for injuries caused by her abusive husband, how many times she had given her the number to shelters for abused woman, and how many lawyers she had recommended to her for use in a divorce. She looked at the woman's face and remembered how innocent and beautiful she had looked the first time she had been brought through the ER's doors, and realized the injuries, stress, and strain of this young woman's life had taken its toll. Chasm felt useless as a medical practitioner in these types of circumstances. She felt her energies begin to surge, swirling and tossing inside of her brain. She looked at the nurse that was attending her patient and said, 'This woman needs to go to the trauma room now!" Chasm recognized the energy that created The Tree of Life coming on, and knew that Tamaria Jackson was its next victim.

Chapter 3
Where Am I Tree of Life?

Tamaria woke up standing in the middle of a long, narrow dark grey cobblestone pathway. She lifted her eyes up and looked ahead of her, in the distance she could see a huge tree with a wooden door hinged to the front of it. Tamaria had the sudden urge to walk towards the tree, it seemed mystically inviting, yet sort of scary. The small amount of fright she felt was not enough to stop her from starting down the path toward the tree. Before she realized what she was doing, or where she was going, she was standing directly in front of a very beautiful door made of Mahogany wooden planks. The grain in each plank was an extravagant puzzle of lines and curves. Tamaria was in total awe of this fabulous tree, she wasn't sure if it was safe to enter, but she was willing to take a chance to see what lay behind the door. She slowly opened the door and walked into the tree. The inside of the tree was nothing Tamaria could ever imagine, a multitude of hallways and doorways. There were dark hallways, bright hallways, long ones, short ones, ones with tall ceilings, ones with short ceilings, and not a single door was the same as another. Tamaria stared around her in complete wordlessness; where was she and how did she find this place? She began to move forward and look at the doors that were closest to her; she came to a very tall and thin one that was the color of a dark forest. The door was the most unusual color green that she had ever seen, it was made of a material that resembled wood, but was actually a very heavy cardboard. As she reached out and tried to turn the gold door knob the door made a loud clicking noise that told her it had just been locked. She jumped back and stared at the door in disbelief and fear, who was behind the door and where had they come from, was the thoughts racing through her mind. Just as she was about to turn tail and run, a very soft whispering wafted across her temples and into her ears, it said to her, "That is not the door for you young miss. No, no, no it is not. There is a hallway with the color of puce, and it is there that you will find a door made of rose vines. Be careful of the thorns when you reach to open it, for they are sharp and painful. This is the way for you to enter your exit, now is the time for you to learn what decisions you will make for your future."

Tamaria was stunned. She turned around and around looking for the person that had spoken to her, but no one was there. Then the voice came to her again, "What are you waiting for? Why do you dawdle? Go, go, go! You haven't much time before I will come to retrieve you, watch for the swirling mist that starts at the top of your head and encompasses you, for it is then that your final decision must be made!"

"Who are you? What are you talking about? I don't understand any of this. Where is this hallway that you speak of?" Tamaria screamed into the empty tree.

"I am The Tree of Many Lives and you are a victim of fate. You must enter the door I have described to you, or never leave this tree. Your lessons are to be learned and your future to be determined. Now go to your right and down the hall with the color of puce, to the door made of rose vines! Take care young lady for yours is a hard path to travel." The tree reverberated through her being.

Tamaria couldn't believe what she was hearing; the tree was talking to her and telling where to go in this maze of doors. She must be dreaming, because this wasn't possible.

29

This kind of thing only happened in the movies, not to her. She decided she would just follow the directions and hope that this dream had a good ending, so she turned to her right and headed down the hallway that appeared to be both blue and purple mixed together. The hall began to get narrower and narrower; it was becoming uncomfortable for her to walk down it. She twisted herself this way and that way to maneuver herself through, but all of a sudden she found herself at an impasse, she could neither go forward nor backward. It appeared as if the hallway had been closing up behind her as she walked, but she had been so intent on getting through it that she hadn't noticed. Oh dear Lord, what was she going to do now? Just then she turned to look and see if there was any way for her to slip down the hallway further, to her astonishment a slightly rounded door made of rose vines appeared. It was a tangled mass of green leaves and light purple rose buds intertwined with dark green and brown vines as thick and round as a child's wrist. On each vine there were large and very sharp thorns poking out in all directions. The handle of the door was a large rose that was also surrounded by thorns. How was she to open this door without getting poked by those horrid pricks? She wondered what was behind this door and why she was to go through it, but since all of it was a dream she figured it really didn't matter. As she reached out to turn the flower knob, the thorns seemed to retreat, and she was safely able to open the door. As she stepped forward, her body began to fall and she instinctively threw her arms and hands out to catch herself on the ground, but there wasn't any ground to be touched. Tamaria was free falling in black empty space. Slowly she began to feel herself lose feeling in her body and her eyesight dimming, then just as she started to panic; consciousness left her. When Tamaria finally landed she sat bolt upright and drew in a huge gasp of air, she opened her eyes and tried to adjust to her surroundings so that she could figure out where she was. She felt something poking her lower back and heard a funny rumble of noise to the right of her, but it was so dark, wherever she had landed, that she could not see her own hand in front of her face. She felt the structure she had landed on, trying to decide what it was; it appeared to be a makeshift padding of some sort. It felt prickly, but it was covered with a soft type of material; probably a sheet or blanket. Reaching behind her she found what seemed to be a pillow; it was covered by the same material that was on the padding underneath her. I'm on a bed? The thought was confusing to her, but it was the only thing that made any sense. What kind

31

of bed was this, and whose bed was it? She began to get worried about the strange whirring and snorting coming from the other side of the bed, what was in the bed with her and how had they come to be here together anyway. The fright of her situation made her shiver so hard that the noise next to her abruptly halted, and there was movement coming towards her. She tried to get out of the bed and run, but she came up hard against a wooden wall and almost knocked herself out.

"OUCH!" she exclaimed in pain. "Waz wrong wit you hunny?" a very masculine, but groggy voice whispered from the other side of the bed. Tamaria almost screamed, only there was no air left in her lungs to form the sound.

"Who are you, where am I?" she whispered back almost in hysterics.

"Jenny, it be me. Yo man Jacob, who you think be in yo bed in da middle of da night?" he said with anger in his voice.

"I'm not Jenny, and you're not my man. What is going on here? I'll scream if you touch me. I want out of here now!" she almost yelled.

"Quiet down now, yo gonna wake up de massa and den all hell gonna breaks loose. Dat musta been some dream yo be havin' fo yo not to knows who I am. It gonna be ok, jes you relax and go backs to sleep," he said soothingly as he wrapped his large arms around her and started to go back to sleep. Tamaria knew something was very wrong, but she was so stunned she didn't have a clue what she could do about it. This man beside her in the bed wasn't hurting her, in fact he was holding her in a firm but caring cradle and he was already back to snoring. No matter how hard she tried to loosen his hold she couldn't, and he didn't seem to budge when she tried to wake him again. After several attempts at escape, she decided to get some rest. The man next to her made that decision easy, because she was tired and he was comfortable to lie next to. She would figure out where she was in the morning; it was then that she would be able to plan her escape. She needed to find a phone so she could call her sister, Natillie was never going to believe all of this; she wasn't even sure she did. As she snuggled into the makeshift bed, her thoughts lingered, before drifting off to sleep, on the warmth and comfort the arms of this big man provided her, and she didn't even know him. She couldn't remember the last time Damien had made her feel so secure.

Chapter 4

History Takes Its Toll

"Mmmmmm, I don't want to wake up. I feel so rested and relaxed," Tamaria said as Damien was lightly shaking her awake.

"Girl, I knows ya don't, but massa gonna be real mad if'n his breakfast ain't on the table on time. I'd like nuttin' better den to lay here in dis bed wit ya and makes ya smile all the day long, but we's got works ta do. It'll jes have ta waits til later." replied a strong voice next to her.

Tamaria quickly sat up and turned to see who had woke her up. There in front of her eyes was the most beautiful man she had ever laid eyes on. He was huge. The bed frame sagged from his weight and size, but it was from pure muscle not fat. This mans arms were the size of small tree trunks, and his chest was a map of bulging muscle. She was in utter shock. His face was the dark, dark color of nighttime and his eyes glowing liquid amber. It was as if Leonardo Da Vinci had carved him from pure onyx, he was a masterpiece of chiseled featuring that would make most grown women melt. It was then that he chose to get out of the bed and grab his pants; she blushed to the roots of her toes at the sight of his bare manliness. Never had she seen such raw male beauty.

"What's wrong wit ya Jenny? Ya acts as if'n ya ain't seed mys bare body befo'!" he said to her with a wink, as he threw some clothes at her. "Now gets yo self dressed befo' Annie gets here to walks up ta the big house wit ya. Ya don wants her ta think we was bein' naughty, does ya!" Jacob said with laughter in his voice.

It was then that she took the time to glance around at her surroundings. She was in some type of wooden cabin, it was very small and had an old antique style wood burning stove in the center of it. The bed she was seated on looked to be made of rough hewn wood, and the mattress was stuffed with hay or grass of some type from the smell of it. There was a hand-made table and two chairs over in the corner, and some old wooden boxes in the other corner that appeared to have bits of yarn, clothe, and thread in them. She had no idea where the hell she was, but she was going to ask this man, that was for sure.

"What's going on here? Where am I? Is this some sort of joke?" she asked Jacob with frustration in her tone.

"Yous been actin' strange all night. Whats ya means is this a joke? This is yo home, and I be yo man! Do ya undastands me? Did ya hits yo head to hard las night when ya wokes me up outa deep sleep? I's goin' to the fields to get workin' befo' de boss man gets mad an beats me. I's hopes ya gets feelin' better befo' I's gets back home." Jacob replied as he turned and opened the rope handled door and walked out. She tried to stop him so she could continue her questioning, but there was a knock at the door before she could reach it. She slowly grasped the rope handle and pulled the door open to see who was there, it was an older black woman with a smile so big it lit up the morning. "Jenny, ya ain't even dressed. Massa gets real mads when we's late, ya knows dat. Come now hurry it ups, we's gots to be getting' the cookin' done. I's wait right here fo ya," the woman said with in an impatient tone of voice, but there was kindness in her eyes. "I'll be out in just a minute," she told the lady and closed the door.

She turned and realized she was totally lost. She had no clue who these people were or where she was, but she knew she had better go along with them if she had any hopes of ever getting back home. So she ran over to the bed and grabbed the clothes that Jacob had thrown to her and started to pull them on. They were old and a bit ragged, but they were clean. There was a muslin undergarment that resembled a slip, but was made of a heavier, courser material, and a long dress that came down past her ankles to drag the floor. The dress was of a dark brown color and buttoned up the front all the way up and along her throat. These were clothes she had seen before, but she couldn't remember where. She looked around and found what must be this "Jenny" person's brush, so she ran it through her hair and made a sort of bun at the back of her head with a wooden rod she had found in one of the sewing boxes. She was as ready as she would ever be. She turned and opened the door to the bright faced woman waiting for her, and walked out into the early morning air ready to meet her fate. All of a sudden she stopped and looked at the woman in front of her, "Where are my shoes?" she asked confused.

"Lawdy, you is a ball of giggles dis mornin', ain't ya! Shoes fo us slaves, lawdy, lawdy ain't dat funny." Annie laughed.

"I don't have shoes." Tamaria said incredulously.

"You quits that now, it be times to get busy an serious. Lets gets us to workin' on the vittles." Annie said, still laughing all the way up the long dirt path as they walked toward the big house. It hit Tamaria like a ton of bricks when the words finally penetrated her brain, SLAVES, she was a slave. That was not possible, there were no more slaves; slavery had ended over a hundred years ago. What was this woman trying to pull; then she looked up from the path and saw the big house for the very first time, and it was then that she realized she had fallen through some sort of time machine and landed in the past. The problem was that she had landed in a time before slavery had been abolished, and she was now some white man's slave girl.

They continued to walk up the steep dirt path straight towards the giant white house at the top. The house sat facing a small stream that seemed to meander its way along the properties boundaries. The four white pillars that ran along the front porch gave the house a bit of a Grecian attitude. It appeared to be a very clean and well kept yard all around the premises. There were bright pink azaleas and purple rhododendrons surrounding the outside walls, and small fern like plants lining the walkway that lead to the front doors. Tamaria couldn't help but think that under different circumstances she would have found this mansion beyond gorgeous. Unfortunately, she was seeing it for the first time as a slave that was kept to maintain its existence. Annie began to turn towards a different trail that lead them to the back of the house, this was the way the slaves entered the kitchen area. Slaves were not permitted to enter their master's homestead through the front entrance, unless the master so deemed it. As they walked up the back stairs and entered the kitchen, Tamaria felt a wave of heat pass over her face and down into every crevice of her bodice. How in the world would she work in this hell's inferno of a kitchen all day? She glanced around and realized that none of the equipment that she was accustom to using in a kitchen setting was available to her; she honestly had no idea what half of the tools were that the other slaves in the kitchen were using. She watched carefully each and every time another tool was taken out of a drawer or off of the wall to see what it was used for. She began to understand what each object represented and very quickly mastered how to use it. A few times one or two of the other cooks would stop and stare at her, as if to say who are you and where did you come from; but not a single one questioned her apparent lack of experience in a kitchen. The day was moving along rather fast, because she found herself doing a multitude of small and large jobs that made time fly by quickly. She had began her day with the cracking of eggs into a large bowl so that Annie could mix together some cornbread for breakfast. Then she was assigned the job of patting out and frying a huge pan full of fresh pork sausage, but as the day progressed so did her duties; until she was standing kneading bread dough for the master's dinner. Although she was absolutely beat, she found a lot of relief in the constant pressure she exerted with every push and pull of the yeasty dough. It was a little therapeutic, helping her to relieve aggressions that were locked up within. She used her quiet time to reflect on what was happening to her and how it had occurred. Tamaria knew that she had been hurt, she remembered the blood on her head, but most of the rest of what had happened to her was a big blur. The only other clue she had was waking up briefly to see the attending emergency room physician looking her over, it was the same lady that kept trying to get her to leave her husband. The doctor was concerned that one of the times Damien beat her up, might be the last time she was capable of taking a breath of air. She really didn't blame the woman doctor for trying to help her out of a dangerous situation, but she also knew that if she left, Damien would hunt her down and kill her. Just as she began to contemplate how mad Damien probably was at this very moment, due to her absence, Annie grabbed her arm and told her it was time to serve up the evening vittles. Tamaria was nervous so she asked Annie, "What do you want me to do?"

Annie looked at her in stunned silence, then replied, "Why whats the massa al'ays has ya doin' at supper time. When Tamaria still stood there with a blank look on her face Annie explained further, "Yous knows what the Massa wants from ya. He wants ya ta serves him and smile alls da while, den he wants ya to thanks him for lettin' yas serve him. When he is done eatin' he be ready to takes ya to his rooms up da stairs. Yous knowed what he does! I's sorry he be infatooaided with yas, buts wes all gots our crosses to bare. Be braves now, and gets in there and gets it over with."

"He takes me up the stairs to his bedroom?" she asked incredulously.

"Yes'm he does, and yous be doin' yas sef' a heap of hurtin' by fightin' him every night. He likes da struggle, jes ya bes calm and gives in real easy like and it won't bes so bad dis time." Annie said with pity.

"Do I get raped by him every night? Do I fight him every night?" Tamaria asked.

"Yep, yous be taken agains' yous will, and yep ya fights da Massa every blessed time."

41

Annie said with confusion in her voice. "Did yous fall or sumptin'? I ain'ts never seed ya actin' so strange and all," she continued. "I's knowed ya hated the Massa's times wit ya an all, but ta act so strange is scarin' the wits outa me."

"I'm sorry if I have you worried Annie, but I seem to have lost a bit of my memory. I woke up from a bad dream last night and slammed my head into the wall rather hard, I think it may be causing me some problems," Tamaria explained. She needed something to blame her weird actions on or this woman was going to call in an exorcist to erase Tamaria's demons!

"I'll try to take your advice tonight, but I can't imagine I will be able to NOT fight the "massa" off of me."

Tamaria walked into the elegant dining room expecting to see a droll little white man sitting and gawking at her while she waited on him hand and foot, but what met her eyes was such a shock to her system that she fainted right there on the spot. As she fell to the carpeted floor in a dead faint, the tray of food she had been carrying slipped out of her grasp and landed with a thud right next to her head. The master of the house stared in disbelief of what had just happened, he knew Jenny hated his touch and advances, but for her to faint was unusual. He rang the bell for his servants to come. When a couple of his stronger male slaves came into the dining room he gestured for them to take the slave girl upstairs to his bedroom.

"Just put her on my bed, it seems to be the only place I get any use out of her anyways," Master Thomas said with sarcasm. "Oh, and make sure she is undressed and ready for me when I come up later."

Chapter 5

The World isn't Always Black and White

Tamaria came to with one thought in her head, how in the world did Darien fall back in time with her? When she had walked into the dining room, she had consigned herself to what she must endure by telling herself it couldn't be any worse than what Darien did to her daily. Then she had looked up and seen Darien sitting at the head of the table, sitting in the master of the plantations chair. Dear God, Darien was the master of this manor. How could that be, he was black, black people can't own black people. What in the world was happening to her, if she was thrown back in time some how using that tree; why was she in the twilight zone?

Tamaria opened her eyes and tried to gain some composure, but the room she was in was very dim. It was lit by a single fireplace in the center of the wall she was facing. She sat up and wondered why she had been taken to a bedroom in the mansion. She was only a slave and she knew from her history classes as a child that slaves were not given these types of quarters to sleep in. She also knew she had woken up next to Jacob in a little slave cabin that was quite a walk from the main house, or big house as it was referred to by Annie, so this couldn't be her bedroom. She slowly swung her legs around in front of her so that they dangled over the edge of the great bed she was sitting on, but her feet never touched the ground. She looked down to see how high up she was and realized this was one of the old fashioned beds she'd seen in the museums, the ones where the women and men who slept in them often had to use a set of stairs to get in and out of them. Tamaria looked all around to find the small set of stairs, but didn't see them anywhere, she would just have to jump and hope she didn't fall on her bottom. She took a deep breath and vaulted herself off of the bed. Amazingly enough she landed flat on her two feet without any problems at all. The door was across the room on the same wall as the fireplace and she had the sudden need to escape this room as fast as possible. A feeling of foreboding was coming over her, and she knew something was wrong.

Just as Tamaria reached the door knob, it began to turn on its own. She jumped back and ran to the other side of the giant four poster bed. She watched to see who was going to come through the door and darn near fainted dead away at the sight of her husband, yet again. Her heart started to flutter and her head felt dizzy, she couldn't seem to get her bearings, why did Darien always affect her so. "Why am I here?" she asked quietly.

"You, my dear little Jenny, are here to please your one and only master, ME!" he replied with conviction.

"What? I don't think I understand what you're asking of me, if you would please explain," she said a little louder, as the fear began to explode in her ears.

"Don't give me that hoity, toity vocabulary of yours. You are supposed be a slave, not a well educated woman. Those people that owned you before I bought you should've never allowed you to learn from there hired school teacher along side their children, as if you were of equal breeding."

"I am sorry if I'm bothersome to your ears, but I will take my leave from your presence if you will only allow me out the door," she said with indignation.

He was across the room in a flash; she never had time to move. He grabbed her by the throat and looked down at her with absolute anger, but it was different than the Darien at home, this Darien had something else in his eyes. It was

46

something she couldn't put her finger on, but it was different, less scary.

"You will address me as Master Thomas, and you will never speak to me with that tone of voice again, or I will cut your tongue out. Do I make myself clear?" he asked with his teeth gritted together.

"Yes sir, Yes sir, Master Thomas. I'm sorry, it'll never happen again, I promise," she said in a whisper, because he was cutting off her air supply with his large hands.

"Get undressed and get up in that bed and wait for me to come back. You had better be ready to do what I say, or you'll regret the day God placed you on this earth!" he yelled at her as he stomped out of the room.

She stood for a second shivering and shaking. What was she to do? On the one hand she had been naked in a bed with Darien many times, so doing it now wasn't a huge deal, but on the other hand this wasn't Darien. True he looked like Darien, and talked like Darien, but his eyes said he was a far cry from the husband she was familiar with. Darien's eyes held nothing but raw hatred of the world, and everything in it. This man's eyes told a different story. Master Thomas showed emotion, he had been angry, in fact down right pissed off, but he had also been hurt and frustrated. His confusion had shown through, as bright as a flashlight in the woods at midnight. She wasn't sure why she had frustrated him so deeply, but she had. She walked over to the bed and looked at it, should she get up in the bed and just pretend it was her husband, or fight him tooth and nail. She thought for a few moments and decided it wouldn't really be cheating on her husband, because she wasn't living in the same time era as him anymore; besides this man might as well have been Darien, no one would be able to tell them apart. She slowly undid her dress and slipped out of it, then dropped the undergarment to the floor along side it. She grabbed a hold of the bedpost at the head of the bed and heaved herself up onto it. She felt a bit like a floozy sitting on the bed totally naked waiting for this man who owned her to come and use her body, so she pulled down the covers and snuggled underneath.

That was exactly how Thomas found Jenny fifteen minutes later when he stepped through the door mumbling to himself that she had better not give him trouble this time. He was sick of fighting this young slave to get what he wanted, slaves were supposed to do what their master told them, not tell them, "no"! He looked over towards the bed and couldn't believe his eyes; she was in the bed sound asleep, and absolutely naked. The covers had fallen off of her shoulders revealing the beautifully rounded breasts that awaited his pleasure. Her face in slumber was almost angelic; her soft dark hair fell in wisps of curls around her face, while her full lips looked as if they had been touched by the morning dew. Those lips were beckoning him to kiss them. He knew he had to be careful not to wake her, or she would start the scratching and screaming like all the other times. He slowly removed his breeches and shirt as he walked on eggshells across the room to the bed. He carefully climbed onto the bed without making a single noise, and then he eased himself under the covers and began caressing her breasts. Oh dear Lord, the soft silky feel of them were pure heaven. He reveled in the moment; never had he been able to truly enjoy this woman's body without the restraints of her arms and legs flaying everywhere trying to stop him. This is how he had always envisioned it would be with Jenny, but she was determined not to betray her husband Jacob, so it was like making love to a cornered cat. He leaned over and took her cinnamon colored nipple in his mouth and began to nibble ever so slightly, not to hard, but enough to send little sparks of electricity to her groin. Jenny began to move and roll. He expected her to come awake and lash out at him trying to kill him, but instead she casually opened her eyes and smiled. "Why did you stop?" she asked in a dreamlike voice. Thomas stared at her in stunned silence. What was wrong with her? Why was she acting like she was enjoying him fondling her? "Hey, are you going to come over here and let me give you a little love, or do I have to come to you?" she continued with a smile that resembled a cat who'd ate a full bowl of fresh cream.

He rolled towards her and grabbed her body up close to him, when she made no move to squirm out of his hold he lowered his head and began to kiss her. She returned the kisses as if she was a starving woman, and they were her sustenance. He reached under her head and pulled her even closer so he could meld their bodies together and deepen the kiss. Their lips were as one and his tongue had no where to go but inside of her mouth. He slowly licked at her lips and the corners of them where they came together to form the heart shaped bow that he had longed to drink from for so long. He slipped his tongue in along the side of hers and they began to wrestle with each others need to make the kiss deeper still.

Tamaria woke to his gentle tugging at her breast, and couldn't help but think how long it had been since Darien had given her so much pleasure, usually it was a quick tug on her panties and a couple of thrusts, then he would roll off of her and go shower with no thought to her needs. She knew this wasn't Darien, but she deserved some pleasure, so she rolled towards him and began her own exploration of his body. Thomas stiffened at first, not sure what to expect from Jenny, but to his great pleasure she began to stroke his back and lightly run her fingers over his buttocks. It felt so sinful, it felt so good that he felt himself stiffen and grow harder than he ever remembered being capable. She felt his response against her thigh and sighed with the thought of what pleasure she would soon be receiving, she had needed this release for a long time now. Thomas gently rolled her on her back and reached between her thighs to caress her womanly nub, it was moist and hot to the touch. He knew she wasn't going to fight him this time, and it was intoxicating to know how good she made him feel. He slowly moved between her thighs and leaned over to take a breast into his mouth again, this time he began to suckle at it like a new born babe. He licked and sucked each of her breasts until the nipples were as hard as his cock. When he knew she could take no more he moved forward and slowly entered her, filling her to the fullest any man ever had. Jenny began to writhe as she felt his huge member enter her, Oh God he was huge; he was much bigger than Darien. She felt the walls of her womanhood expand and stretch to take him all, and he felt so good. Reaching around the back of his head she drew him down for a long and very deep kiss, exploring every crevice of his mouth. He began to move in and out of her taking her to unbelievable heights of excitement. She started to moan and cry out; he looked down at her and whispered, "Am I hurting you?" He wasn't sure why it mattered to him, but it did, this time it did.

In between gasps for air she tried to tell him that he was far from hurting her, that he was just driving her crazy with desire.

"I want you to make me loose my mind. I want to feel you pound yourself inside of me until we both burst. I need you to make me feel like a woman tonight, please," were the words that she managed to get out. Thomas needed no more encouragement he threw himself into the passionate moment and began to ram his cock inside of her as deep as he could, and she moved her hips up and down to meet his every thrust. They were a writhing mass of sexual pleasure. When neither could stand the constant need for more they grabbed each other and climaxed at the exact same moment; Thomas with a loud animal growl, and Tamaria with Darien's name on her lips.

"Who the Hell is Darien!" Thomas asked with clenched teeth.

Before she could answer Thomas he was up and off of the bed ready to do battle if his stance was any indication. She watched him as he paced back and forth in the room looking at her through his marvelously long dark eyelashes. He was a thing of beauty; his every movement a liquid motion in balance with each individual muscle his body used. He was the color of the hard shell on a walnut and his hair was the dark black of midnight; he kept it closely cropped to his head, which only emphasized his glorious facial featuring. The strong squared jaw line, that was clenched in anger, but still very appealing. The almond shaped dark brown eyes, which seemed to look straight through you and see a person's inner core. The nose very prominent on his face, but straight with just enough of a flair in the nostrils to give a bit of a classical good look to the rest of his features. The one thing she was continually drawn back to, and the reason she had been so attracted to the Darien she had married, were the fabulous lips on this man's face. They were like no others she had ever viewed; full, but only enough to make a woman want to touch them with her fingers to see if they are real; slightly darker than his skin tone, as if they had been painted by Michelangelo himself; and so soft that once you've felt them against your own, one could never stop wanting that feeling over and over again. She knew he was about to explode from the lack of her answer to his question, but she wasn't sure how to answer him. If she told him the truth he'd think her crazy, but if she lied she risked getting caught in that lie and punished for her insolence. She finally decided to give a half truth, "Darien was the name of my father. I'm sorry for saying it during our time of, of well, pleasure, but you reminded me of him a great deal tonight when you walked into this room telling me what I was going to do and how I was to do it. My father was a very controlling man, which kept a tight leash on me. It must have been on my mind more than I had thought, because in the heat of the moment Master Thomas didn't seem the right words to yell," she said hoping he took her bait and grew indignant that he should remind her of a father figure during their love making, it was all she could think of at such short notice.

"I remind you of a controlling father? I remind you of your strict daddy? How is that? You were very receptive to my advances tonight, am I to believe you were as giving of your body when it came to pleasing your father, as you were to me this evening?" he almost growled at her. She realized she had made a big mistake as soon as the words had left her mouth, but it was too late to retract them so she tried to explain a little better, "On the other plantation my missus and master believed that the slaves should care for their families as if they were no different than white people. My Daddy was of the mind set that I was a very delectable piece of woman flesh and that many of the young black slaves would try to get me to be with them, so he was very mean and controlling. He walked me to and from the big house when I had my classes with the master's children and he never let me out of his sight unless my older brother was around to take over. If he even thought I'd gotten away without any supervision, he would beat me and lock me in the shed for the night to punish me. You reminded me of him when you tried to strangle me," she finished a little out of breath. She sat and waited for his reply, but really she waited to see if he would believe her or try to kill her. Tamaria realized how close to the truth she had just come as she sat and waited; her father had been named Darien; he had treated her like a piece of property not a daughter to love and cherish, but a whore to sell to the highest bidder. How funny to finally see the connection between her father and her husband of the future after all of the years of abuse she had withstood.

"Look Jenny, JENNY, are you listening to me?" he asked in a stern voice.

Tamaria jerked as she pulled herself out of thought and realized she was the Jenny he was talking to; it was taking some time getting used to being called Jenny instead of her real name Tamaria. "Yes, I'm listening to you. I was just a little lost in the memories of my past, that's all," she replied quietly.

"Jenny, I am your master and I know we have not had the best of relationships, with the fighting and all the force I've used in the past, but I would like that to change. I will always be your master that will never change, but the anger and animosity does not have to stay the same. As long as you are more accepting of the fact that you will be in this room to please me when I require it to be so, then we can have many more evenings like we just shared. I know you enjoyed our love making as much as I, so I propose to make a truce, if only in this bedroom,"

he said with a question in his voice.

"What about Jacob?" she asked.

"Jacob is a slave! He will deal with whatever I hand him and smile. If he were to try and cause trouble for me or get in the way of what I want, I would simply sell him! Would you like me to have to sell him?" he threatened.

"NO! You can't do that, he hasn't did anything wrong. Leave Jacob alone," she yelled at him. Tamaria wasn't sure what the relationship was between Jenny and Jacob, but by the way he had spoken to her this morning she knew it was one of love, so she couldn't let Master Thomas hurt Jacob.

"Jacob is replaceable. If you want to keep him here with you in whatever capacity you two have agreed to live with one another, then you had better agree to be complacent to all my wishes. Is that understood?"

Tamaira felt anger well up in her, how could he be such a hateful asshole after all the beauty they had just shared. "Yes, I understand completely, you are exactly what I had originally thought; you are my father just in a different form," she spat out at him like venom from a snakes fangs. Thomas marched over to the bed and grabbed her shoulders to draw her close to him; he slowly leaned into her and gave her a searing deep kiss. She struggled to pull away, but he forced her to remain a part of the whole charade until she began to feel warm and almost liquid inside. He pulled away

57

from her abruptly and said with a sneer, "Never compare me with such filth as your father again, or I will show you further how much you want to be with me; fighting what you desire is not easy. I will not deal with the insult of your father lightly!" he finished as he turned and walked to the door. "For God's sake get dressed and remove yourself from my rooms before I return, you disgust me. Go back to your Jacob with the smell of me on your body and let him know how it feels to want!" he left her as he walked out of the room. She sat in stunned silence. The dirty feeling that crawled over her skin was a familiar one, one that she often had felt after being forced to have sex with Darien. What was fate playing here, what cruel game was she being placed in? She quickly got up and dressed herself, then quietly left Master Thomas' room. Tamaria slipped down the hall trying to find the staircase that lead downward, finally she saw a little narrow stairwell that went down so she followed it. The stairs lead her to the back of the house where the kitchen was located. As she came through the door way Annie was waiting for her, "Oh, my po' sweet hunny chile. Was it so bad dis times to? Comes wit me an wes get ya all cleaned ups and backs home ta yo' man Jacob," she said to Tamaria while she ushered her out of the big house and down a little path to a large well. Annie pulled a bucket of water out of the well and dabbed her apron in it to moisten it, then she turned and had Tamaria sit on the side of the well while she gently wiped off the tears that had been falling from her eyes. Tamaria hadn't even realized that she was crying, everything had happened so fast that she had just hurried to leave the room without trying to gage her own emotions to the situation. It was the first time she had cried in years. The tears had stopped very soon after the beatings had begun with Darien. She had learned that it only made things worse and soon she had become numb to the pain anyways. Damn Master Thomas for making her feel again, she thought as a fresh set of tears began there trek down her face. She remained still all the while that Annie was cleaning her up and gently whispering words of comfort.

"Annie, what will Jacob think of me and of what I've done?" she said dejectedly.

"Hunny chile, Jacob don' needs to knows what be goin' ons in dat house of hell. I won' tells him ifin' yous don'," she said with a kind smile.

"Wes' wimmons has ta stick together an dats what I plans on doin', K?" she continued.

"Thank you for being my friend Annie, I am so grateful for all of your help," Tamaria said as she reached over and hugged the large black woman.

"Oh, nows ya imbarasssin' an ole' woman!" Annie laughed as she hugged Tamaria back.

It felt so good to be hugged simply because someone cared about her, Tamaria didn't want to let go of Annie but before long she had to, because it was time to face Jacob.

Chapter 6
Time to Face the Music

Tamaria waved goodbye to Annie as she slowly walked up the steps of the little cabin she was to live in while she remained in this time warp. How was she going to hide what had happened between her and the master? How did Jenny hide it every day of her life? She was gaining a real sense of the woman that was within the body she had been thrown into. Jenny must have a true love for the man she slept next to every night, how else could she endure the abuse that she went through daily from Master Thomas; never telling Jacob about any of it. Jenny must be a strong willed and strong minded woman to fight for her virtue every single time that evil demon touched her, and still be able to freely give her body to another man; never feeling betrayed or dirty. Tamaria wished she had more of Jenny's strength inside of her. Where had it gone, how had she lost that pride and love of herself over the lifetimes? Tamaria slowly opened the door that lead inside the cabin in hopes that Jacob would be asleep and she would not wake him. It was dark outside and she knew he worked in the fields during the day, so he might be asleep. As she undressed herself and pulled her night dress over her head a gentle voice came to her from the direction of the bed, 'Jenny, where's ya been? It be late. That Master Thom be workin' yous later and later each day. Hurries up I's been waitin' on ya, I's been missin' my sweet Jenny all days long."

"I'll be right there Jacob. I'm just getting in my night stuff," she said hoping the nervousness wasn't in her voice.

She finished getting dressed for bed and grabbed the brush she had found earlier in the morning to run it through her hair. She was stalling for time. Tamaria knew Jacob wanted to make love, but she wasn't sure she would be able to after what had just occurred between her and Master Thomas. She wasn't sure she could be with another man other than her husband, it had been a long time since she had even thought about it. With Master Thomas it was different, she could imagine that he was Darien, and nothing seemed too unusual. True Master Thomas had actually taken the time to pleasure her as well as him, but it wasn't always bad between her and Darien so she could accept that. Jacob was a very different situation; it wasn't that she didn't find him attractive, because she did. He was a very manly man, with muscle and strength that exuded from his very skin, but that was what she was most afraid of. What if he found out about Master Thomas and her, would he beat her for not telling him? She had taken a lot of abuse over her years, but she truly believed if this man tried to hit her she wouldn't ever get back up.

Tamaria carefully climbed over top of Jacob to get inside the bed, as she was adjusting the cover and trying to lie down as far away from him as possible he reached over to caress her face. His hands were gentle as they glided over the planes of her face, only stopping when they reached her mouth. Tamaria was so moved by this gentle gesture of love that before she knew what she was doing she had kissed his fingers. Jacob pulled her close to him and just held her. He stroked her back and shoulders with those wonderfully large hands so very lightly that she began to get goose bumps up and down her arms. Slowly he moved lower and began to stroke the backs of her thighs and her buttocks. The feeling of complete safety and euphoria enveloped Tamaria and all thought of Master Thomas left her mind. She was safe and loved, and it felt wonderful. Instinctively, she began to realize that Jacob would never make her do anything she didn't want to. Jacob loved Jenny, it was really that simple, and when you love someone you do not try to hurt them. Tamaria decided right then and there that if she was going to be stuck in Jenny's body, she might as well enjoy the benefits, as well as the detriments Jenny received on a daily bases. She snuggled closer to Jacob and soaked up all the gentle loving he was willing to give. He started to kiss her forehead and eyelids, then he moved his head down and began to kiss her neck; she was about to come unglued. She couldn't believe her own body, it was reacting like a dried up old sponge that had been thrown into water. How could she get so excited so quickly after making love to Master Thomas? That was her last coherent thought, as Jacob moved all the way down her belly with small ticklish kisses and slowly spread her legs to taste what was between them. Jacob began to lick and suck at her woman parts with such an expertise she almost reached her climax after only a couple of minutes of his attention. She quickly grabbed his head and pulled him upwards to stop the insanity. She wanted to please him and make him know how much Jenny loved him, so she pushed him down on the bed to lie on his back and began to kiss his stomach, until she reached the coarse hairs of his private parts, and then she gently took hold of his rather impressive erection and began to lick and suck him. She couldn't take all of him into her mouth, because he was too large and she would choke, but she stroked the base of his manhood as she kissed him and pleasured him. Tamaria felt the intake of breath as Jacob took it, she knew he had not experienced this sort of pleasure from Jenny by his reaction. The fact that it was her and not Jenny that was bringing him such happiness gave her a feeling of pure satisfaction that she knew was probably wrong, but she didn't care. She could tell he was about to explode by the constant moans and movement of his legs beneath her. Jacob was almost past the point of endurance, what was Jenny doing? She had never given him this type of pleasure before and he wasn't sure if he could take much more, but it felt so good. If she didn't stop it soon, he would loose himself into her mouth. He gently placed his hand on her head and stopped her from moving, "Jenny, if's yous keeps that up I'm gonna embarrass mys self," he said breathlessly. "Come here an gives yo man a chance ta makes ya smile."

Tamaria let Jacob lay her on her back and position himself between her thighs. When Jacob began to fill her womanhood with his large member Tamaria felt like she would explode from the sheer girth of it, but the length reached the very depth of her soul. It was painful to say the least, and before she could stop herself she let out a tiny gasp. Jacob stopped in the middle of entering her, "Are yous okay, am I hurtin' ya?' he asked with concern.

"No, it's just that, well I'm a bit tense and need you to go a little slower, that's all," she said as her body started to accommodate his size.

"Oh, I'm so sorry Jenny, I's just got so excited from yous lovin', I forgots how tiny yous is!" he said with remorse.

"No Jacob, you don't have to apologize. I love you and you feel soooo good, it's me that is having trouble relaxing; not you."

He relaxed when he heard the sincerity in her voice and began to slowly fill her again. When he had finally filled her with the whole of him, he stayed very still and just kissed her with all his passion; until she had time to get mildly used to the feel of him. Tamaria had never been loved quite so completely in all of her life. As she got used to the feeling of him she started to feel a fire start in her loins, she became aggravated that he was being so careful with her. She needed him to move inside her and keep filling her with his manliness. Jacob was trying to hold back so he wouldn't hurt Jenny, but all he really wanted to do was pound himself inside of her as deep as she would let him. When Tamaria reached behind Jacob and grabbed his buttocks to pull him closer, he almost came undone. "I don's want ta hurts ya Jenny?" he said questioningly.

"It's okay now Jacob, I'm all relaxed and want you to make love to me anyway you want to. I want to please you in whatever way you need me," she said knowing it was all he needed to let go and make her wild with want.

Jacob couldn't believe his ears, Jenny had always been so tender and wanted him to go slow when it came to love making, but he wasn't looking a gift horse in the mouth. Jacob started to move in and out of her with such skill that Tamaria could barely breathe. With each long hard stroke of his cock, she became crazier for him. The need to be fulfilled over came her and she started to move beneath him meeting his every thrust with a thrust upwards from her hips. It was a sweet, sweet pleasurable pain to be filled to the very core. When her body could no longer take the onslaught of his manhood, and his manhood could no longer take the utter abandon of pleasure; they exploded in a giant gasp of fulfilled needs. The climax was like nothing she had ever experienced; she wasn't sure how she was going to be capable of walking the next morning, but she didn't care it was all to good to let go of. Jacob rolled off of her and pulled her tight to him, he whispered, "I loves ya hunny," and promptly fell asleep. Tamaria sighed with the feeling of happiness that enveloped her when she was in Jacob's arms and soared into a wonderful sleep of her own. For once she wasn't worried about anything.

The next morning while sweat was dripping down Tamaria's under garments and soaking her clothes from the intense heat of the little kitchen off of the big house's dining room area, she found herself deep in thought. She needed to find out exactly where and when she was in time. It was very hot and humid where ever it was, but when she was in the kitchen cooking it was stifling. She didn't know how these women handled the heat and hard work without passing out from sheer exhaustion. The night she had spent with Jacob had started her thinking about what she had been missing out on in her own marriage back home. Tamaria was jealous of the woman Jacob called Jenny. She knew this life was really nothing to be jealous of with the hard labor, lecherous slave owners, and lack of complete freedom, but somehow the total love of a good man made all the bad seem minute in comparison. If Darien were to treat her in the kind and loving manner that Jacob treated Jenny, Tamaria would be in heaven. She wasn't sure what she was going to do when it came to leaving this place, but she knew it would be a little harder to leave now that she had discovered the happiness she could share with Jacob if she stayed. However, that didn't include the problems she had to face with Master Thomas, those were problems she was unwilling to allow to mar her beautiful memories of the night with Jacob. She was busy cracking eggs and mixing up the dough for the days bread when she heard footsteps come up behind her, then before she could turn to see who was there a set of strong hands were wrapped around her and caressing her breasts.

"What the Hell!" she exclaimed in surprise.

"It's just little ole' me Jenny. I thought you would remember the feel of my hands on your flesh from yesterday?" Thomas said with a leer in his voice.

"Leave me be. I'm busy making the food for your table. Unless you're not hungry today, I suggest you leave me to my work," was her reply.

"Why you're blushing, but whatever for? I've not only stroked and pleasured every inch of your body; I've also seen each piece of beauty!"

69

"Pleasure is not exactly what I would call what you were attempting with me; controlling me, forcing me, and degrading me would be much more appropriate terms."

"Look here you little wench; I will not tolerate your disobedience in any way. I am the Master of this house and you are nothing more than a slave girl who can be used and thrown away whenever the mood hits me, or perhaps sold to the most despicable individual I can find," Thomas threatened.

"Your threats are no good. Getting as far away from you as I can would only give me the so called pleasure you thought you had given me in your bedroom!" she said between clenched teeth. When Tamaria glanced back to see the effect her words had created on Master Thomas' face she realized she may have gone to far.

"You must not be thinking clearly, my girl, because it is not just you that I can sell."

As Thomas walked away Tamaria almost shuttered from the intensity with which he had spewed his threats. Why would he threaten to sell someone else to hurt her? Who was he referring to anyways? This was not going to be a very easy day, and she had caused more trouble for herself through her own insolence. She couldn't help it, whenever that man came within six feet of her she wanted to either kill him or run.

As the day wore on Tamaria started to get into the routine that was the kitchen slaves' life. It was constant work. First the breakfast had to be made and served which consisted of: homemade flapjacks, French toast, freshly scrambled eggs, bacon, sausage, biscuits made that same morning, gravy that Annie made from the bacon and sausage fat, whatever fruit that was capable of harvesting (today it was strawberries she had picked from the gardens), toast with freshly churned butter, and last but not least juice, coffee, and milk from the farm cows. This plantation was huge and had everything that was necessary to live contained within the boundaries of the plantation property lines. When breakfast had been served it was then time to clean all the dining room furniture, dishes from breakfast, and the entire kitchen while starting the preparations for lunch. Cleaning in this kitchen was very different from what Tamaria was accustomed to, she had to go outside and down the path to the well where she drew in a couple of wooden pails of water and carried them back up the path to the kitchen. One of the pails was then placed in a large caldron and heated until it was steaming hot, then poured into a wooden basin of sorts where it was mixed with

71

soap and used for washing the dishes. The other pail was left cold and used for rinsing the soap off of the cleaned dishes. There were no scrubbing pads only a wire brush that was used for the large pots and pans. The concept of a dishwasher wasn't even a twinkle in someone's eye yet. The floors had to be swept and scrubbed with a large scrub brush. Once again Tamaria found herself walking down to the well to get water for the floors. She was so tired already she felt like her legs were becoming noodles. Good God in heaven, how in the world did these women survive one full day of this torturous labor; much less an entire lifetime? Tamaria was really beginning to get homesick. She sat down on the side of the well trying to figure out what she must do next. She had to scrub the floors, then start a pot of boiling water over the cooking fire for the chicken that Annie was braising, then she needed to get some dumplings made, and there was also the okra that needed fetching from the cellar; this was only for lunch what the heck was going to be served for supper!

A soothingly soft sound wafted through the air towards Tamaria's ears as she sat and contemplated the rest of the day's chores; it was a lovely melody that she had never heard before. The song was coming from up the trail a ways where she couldn't see the source; it made her want to know who was capable of whistling such beautiful music. Almost as if her thoughts were heard, Jacob came walking around the bend and heading straight towards her and the well. She watched as he casually headed in her direction, and the smile that had come over his entire face when he had seen she was at the well. A more beautiful man she had never seen and she doubted she ever would have the fortune to see again, after leaving this time zone. How lucky she was to have at least one person in this nasty nightmare that she could look forward to seeing everyday, but more than seeing she looked forward to touching this man. Once again she sat in awe of his huge and muscular body, the strength behind those muscles could break through a brick wall, yet he was so gentle when he made love to her. The sheer size of him could suffocate her, and still his agility and compassionate nature would not allow him to do such things. She was so happy to see him that she forgot all of her pain and exhaustion and stood to walk down the trail to meet him.

"Oh Jacob, you are a sight for sore eyes!" she exclaimed as she reached out to place her arms around him in a large hug.

"Jenny, it be so good to sees ya. I never espected to comes across yas here at this times o' day, but I's sure glad I's did. I ain't been ables to stop thinkin' on what we's done last night," he said with a slight blush to his cheeks. It was so endearing to see this giant of a man blush over their lovemaking the night before that she could not stop her urge to reach up and kiss him.

"Jacob, you are the one reason at this time in my life that I find to go on living. God must love me to send you here to watch over me and love me," she said in a breathless voice.

"Jenny ya sure is actin' strange lately, buts I's ain't complainin' cause I likes it!" Jacob said with a smile so wide she thought he'd split his whole face in half.

"I had better get this water back up to the big house and get busy doing my work so I can get home early tonight and give you something else to think on all day tomorrow!" Tamaria said with a wink and a grin.

Jacob just stared at her in complete speechlessness. He couldn't believe his ears. "Yo be such a naughty gal, Jenny, but I likes it!" he laughed as she walked away. She could still hear him giggling as she started up the stairs into the kitchen.

Tamaria's thoughts were of Jacob and how much easier the work would be now that she had something to look forward to as she brought the buckets in the kitchen; she never expected to find Master Thomas waiting on the roughly hewn wooden stool that was set by the fire for Annie when she was busy stirring and cooking over it. "Well, well did you have a nice afternoon rendezvous with that big buck? I hope you put his face in your permanent memories, because I have a few men that are very interested in buying him for stud on their plantations; in fact they're coming here tomorrow to check him out. I figure once he is no longer a concern for you, you will be able to concentrate on your behavior towards me," he said to her with absolute pleasure. Tamaria couldn't breath, she felt like a large boulder had just slammed into her chest. Oh God, he couldn't do this, he just couldn't. Jacob didn't deserve to pay for her sins, and truthfully she just couldn't handle living in this time era without him. She calmed down enough to see he was looking for her reaction and she knew she mustn't give him what he wanted.

"What does it matter to me what you do with any of these people on this plantation?"

"Oh it matters; I saw the shock that just ran through you."

"Shock, well of course, I can't quite figure out why you would sell one of your better and more amicable slaves just to get me upset. I am not sure what this will gain for you, but a less capable work force," she replied as nonchalant as she was able to do.

Master Thomas was trying to gage how much of her reactions were shock and how much of them were emotional pain. He wanted to hurt her the way she had hurt him this morning with her claims of disinterest and lack of pleasure from their sexual escapades.

"I want to get rid of whatever men may be taking what is rightfully mine. That is the reason for my selling Jacob, or am I wrong in assuming that the two of you are fucking in that little shack you call home."

"I am no ones property no matter the circumstances. If you want my body then of course you shall receive it, but you can not force my mind or heart to love any man; including yourself!" she told him with conviction. "I was bought and brought to this plantation, and have set out to make my life as easy as I am capable of doing ever since. If living in a shack with Jacob gives me some comfort then I will do it, but make no mistake, I rule who I love and want to be with," she finished with. Tamaria hoped that Master Thomas believed everything she was telling him, it wasn't true, but if it got him to leave Jacob alone then it was worth it. Unfortunately, she had no idea that Jacob had followed her up the trail, after cleaning up from working in the fields that afternoon.

"Jacob, is there something I can do for you?" Master Thomas asked with a cenacle grin on his face.

"No sir, I's was jest bringin' Mis Jenny her apron, she lefts it down by the well whens she cames to get da water fo' the flo's'" Jacob replied dejectedly.

"Well then give it to her," Thomas told Jacob.

Jacob walked over and handed the apron to Tamaria and gave her the coldest glare she had ever felt. She tried to convey to him her apologies through her touch, but he pulled away before she could grasp his hand.

"I'lls be on mys way now, thank ya Masser Thomas."

"No problem Jacob, I'll need to talk with you tomorrow about a little opportunity I have that concerns you, so come to see me before you go out to the fields in the morning."

"Yes sir, Masser Thomas, I's be here bright an early," Jacob said and then quickly left the kitchen area.

"You Bastard, how could you do that to him," she screamed as soon as Jacob had gone.

"Why Jenny, I thought you didn't give one hoot for Jacob? What's this I hear in your voice, would that be concern? You had better listen up and listen good, if you want to keep your little buck here and in your bed you had better damn well be taking care of my every need, and I do mean every!"

"What do you want from me?"

"Every time I walk into a room and you are present I want you to fall all over yourself to show how much you want me and how much pleasure you gain from our encounters. Also you will not udder a word of disrespect towards me; ever! Do you understand me, can you comprehend what I am saying to you?" he said matter-of-factly.

"Yes, but only if you leave Jacob alone and allow us the peace of one another while we are in our cabin alone," she replied.

"You are demanding something of me? That is interesting considering my position and what I can do to your so-called-life, but I like your feisty nature so I will allow you that one request. However, if you step out of line even one time, Jacob will be off to another plantation where he will be making lots of little slave babies with as many women as his new owner tells him to breed with. Do we understand one another my little concubine?" he asked, never really expecting a reply, but he got one.

"I understand you more than you realize, so yes *Masser Thomas I's be a good little slave gal, I's promises I will!*" she said mimicking the normal talk of slaves on the plantation.

Master Thomas allowed her this one last insolence and walked out of the room.

What in the world was she going to do now, Tamaria wondered nervously? Jacob thought she was only using him, and he now knew she had been having sex with Thomas; what a mess. She had to find a way to get Jacob to understand why she had said the things she had said, and that the sex was something forced upon her by Master Thomas. Tamaria knew the rest of the day that had seemed so much better since seeing and talking to Jacob; would now be spent worrying over how she could fix this situation.

Chapter 7

Considering Jenny

At dinner that night Master Thomas ignored Tamaria's presence. It was obvious that he wasn't going to require her to please him that evening. He spent most of the evening yelling at the kitchen help and trying to act as if he didn't want Tamaria near him. Tamaria was happy that she wasn't going to have to go upstairs and deal with the Master's needs; she wanted to rectify the problems that he had created for her and Jacob. The problem was that she wasn't exactly sure what she could do or say to make the situation better. As the evening wore on she became more and more apprehensive about facing Jacob, which was when she finally realized that Master Thom had ignored her on purpose. He wanted to send her home to deal with Jacob as soon as possible, he wanted to let Jacob punish her and wait to see the results. She was not enjoying this time in her life, she wasn't prepared to deal with one insanely jealous and mean man, much less two of them.

While she finished up the cleaning in the kitchen with the other house slaves, Tamaria thought hard and long on the situation that Jenny had been dealing with all the time she had been on this plantation. The only joy that Jenny had was her love of a sweet and tender man, but even that was tainted by her nightly dealings with Master Thomas. How in the world did she do it? As Tamaria slowly walked down the path towards Jenny and Jacob's home, she was lost in her thoughts and didn't hear Annie talking to her. "Jenny, hey gal', JENNY!" Annie said a little louder.

Tamaria came out of her dazed and confused thought processing and realized Annie had been speaking to her.

"What, oh I'm sorry, I was just thinking Annie. What did you say?"

"Gal, yo's been so strange lately's that I don' even knows who yo be any mo's?" she said questioningly.

"Annie, I don't know who I am anymore than you. Earlier this afternoon Jacob came up to the kitchen to bring me my apron I had left down by the well, and he over heard Master Thom and I having an argument. He also heard me refer to what Master Thom does with me after dinner," she said as if in confession with a priest.

"Oh dear Lords, dear Lords! What's did Jacob say?"

"He just looked at me like he hated me and told Master Thom he'd be back up to the big house in the morning. You see I was telling the Master that Jacob didn't mean two hoots to me when he over heard our conversation, but I was only acting that way to stop him from trying to sell Jacob!"

"He be going to sells Jacob? Whys would he wants to's do that?"

"He wants him out of his way with me, he thinks I'll be more receptive to his wants if Jacob were to be removed from the picture," Tamaria sobbed. "I am so lost in this place, Annie; I don't even know where I am. How can fix all this mess?"

"Chile yo's in Savannah Gorgia' and yo' not lost yo wit fren's and family. I'll hep ya as bests as I's knowd how, dat I's promises," Annie said with conviction. "It be wrong ta treats peoples the ways dat Massa Thom be doin', him bein' black an' all hissef."

"Thank you Annie, I don't know what I'd do without you. Do you know what year it is Annie, I can't seem to remember?" Tamaria asked hopeful that she might find out what time frame she had fallen into.

"Sho' it be 1842, hunny. Is yo sick?"

"No Annie, I'm just confused," Tamaria said quietly.

"Well, we's be at yo' house. Goot lucks wit yo man, yo tells him nots ta be mean an all, tells him Annie says so," Annie said as she continued down the path towards her own home.

Tamaria knew she had to figure out what to do, but there wasn't any time left to waste, she was home. She opened the door and walked inside, there was an old oil lamp lit on top of one of the wooden crates by the table, and Jacob was sitting in a chair by the run down wood burning stove. He turned as she walked in and looked at her through pain filled eyes; he resembled a puppy that had just been kicked. Tamaria's heart skipped a beat at the hurt she knew she had caused this man; it was then that she realized she didn't belong to this man and he didn't belong to her. Jacob was Jenny's man and it was so wrong for Tamaria to try and take her place. She had to try and explain what was happening and help Jacob fix this horrible situation he and Jenny were in. Even though she wanted nothing more than to walk over to Jacob, sit down on his lap, and wrap herself in his comforting nature; she knew in the end it wasn't really Jacob that she wanted to comfort her. Tamaria wanted to go home to her real life and walk up to Darien and gain the feelings she had been given by Jacob's caring nature. She wanted to go back in time and fix the horrid things that had caused Darien to be so filled with hate. She realized that this might be the only chance she had to do that; the tree had seen this need in her and given her the opportunity to find and fix Darien's problems. She had been so lost in the feelings of security, safety, and love, that she had almost missed out on a once in a lifetime gift.

Tamaria walked over to Jacob with as much bravado as she could muster, "Look Jacob, I am truly sorry about what happened up at the big house, but I wasn't trying to hurt you. I was trying to stop Master Thomas from selling you. I know you probably hate me, but that's fine if it helps you to understand what I'm about to tell you. Please listen carefully, it may be hard to understand what I'm going to try and explain."

"Massa Thom be's ready ta sells me?" Jacob finally got out.

"Yes, he WAS ready to sell you. He is jealous of what we have between us and wanted to hurt me by getting rid of you, but that isn't important anymore. I stopped him, he has promised not to sell you and to leave you and Jenny be when you are alone in this little cabin. Now we have to figure out how to stop him from using Jenny for his little play thing so you two can be happy. Well as happy as two slaves can possibly be," Tamaria finished.

"Whats be ya talkin' about Jenny? All dis talks likes yo ain't even yo'sef. I be worried abouts ya. Why didn' yas tell me abouts the Massa forcin' his'sef on ya, Jenny, why? I's wouda undrestoods, I's woulda been mo' carefuls wit ya, not espectin' so much froms ya at night an all. I's love ya Jenny," Jacob proclaimed.

"Jacob, listen I'm not your Jenny, my name is Tamaria Jackson. I am from the year 2003. I live in Savannah, Georgia on a little street called Miracle Avenue, in a cute little three bedroom home with my husband Darien. Our marriage is not what anyone could call perfect, but I think I can make it much better with your help. I can also help with Jenny having to give in to master Thomas. I know it sounds strange, but I swear its true. I was in a hospital room, and then in front of a tree, and then I woke up in your bed. I didn't even know what year it was or what state I was in until an hour ago."

Jacob just sat and stared at Tamaria as if she were a demon. He slowly swallowed and tried to come to some semblance of sanity. Jacob thought about the other night when Jenny had woke him up and ran herself right into the wall, just like

85

she wasn't familiar with her own home. Then there was their lovemaking the other night, Jenny was always so shy and hesitant, but that night she had been so bold with him that he had thought she was possessed. Now the way she was talking was so strange, but if what she was saying had even a tiny bit of truth in it, it would explain all the strange things that had been happening with Jenny.

Tamaria looked at Jacob and thought he was probably trying to figure out how to get out of the cabin and away from the psycho woman that she sounded like, she knew she was taking a large risk in telling him the truth, but the tree had told her she had a very short time before it came back for her. She had wasted to much of it just sitting around trying to be Jenny. God help her she hoped Jacob was willing to forgive her, and help her figure out Master Thomas. Tamaria knew in her heart that if she did not figure out where all of Master Thomas' hatred began, that she would walk right back into her future life and not be able to make the changes necessary for her to survive her marriage to Darien. It was strange the clarity that overtook Tamaria; suddenly she understood, suddenly she knew exactly why this time travel thing had happened to her. The tree was a portal of truth, it helped those people that hid from there selves to open up and search out what the difference was between reality and what they deemed there existing lives. She knew, although it did not seem like it at the moment, that this was a very special gift given to her by God above and a very special tree that he had created. Jacob was staring at her from across the little cabin with utter confusion, but she also realized that he was trying to see if what she had told him might be true. Jacob slowly stood up and walked the few steps that separated them, he reached across to Tamaria and felt her face; very gently he caressed the face he had loved for the past years he and Jenny had been together. How could it be possible that this face that so looked like his Jenny was really some other woman that came from the future?

"Jenny, or Tammarra, whoever yo' be, I's havin' a bit o' trubble wit dis. I's knowed somthin' wrong when yo' be so relaxd' da other nigh', but yo look an' talks jes likes my Jenny? I wants to believes ya, but how can I's?" Jacob said in a quiet and confused voice. He was so lost. He had no idea how any of this could actually happen. His first thought was of some voodoo lady having cast a horrible curse on him and Jenny, but he did not know any such person and he had not done anything to deserve such a curse; nor had Jenny. Jacob kept staring at Tamaria trying to see if there was at least a tiny difference between her and Jenny, and that is when he noticed that the mole Jenny had always had under her chin, just below the jaw line, was missing. He almost jumped for joy.

"Okay, I's believes ya', yo' not my Jenny," he stated simply. Tamaria looked at him in stunned shock, "What made you believe me?" she asked incredulously.

"Yo's don' haves the tiny litt'l mole on yo chin likes my Jenny. I's can'ts believes I missed it fo so long, but I's did. Musta been da shock o' yo' unusual ways o' doin' things," he replied.

Then it seemed to hit him that he had not only been sleeping with this stranger, but he had been intimate with her as well, what was he going to tell Jenny?

"Oh my Gods', whats has I's don'? Jenny goin' ta leaves me fo' sure. I's was unfateful' ta her," he almost cried at Tamaria. "What's I's goin' ta do's?"

"Look Jacob, it's okay, if I understand what is going on, then you don't not have to worry. Jenny will return to this life when I go back to mine and never know she left it. It will be as if you were with her the whole time. She won't be asking any questions and you should not volunteer any answers, do you understand me?"

"How's dat?" he asked perplexed.

"I've been sent here to learn a few things about the husband in my future life through Master Thomas, but Jenny was only removed for the small time I was sent here. Jenny is me from a past life, so she is now me in my future life. I was beaten by my husband and left unconscious in my living room, when they found me and took me to the hospital, a healing place; I went into a coma and..."

"Whats a coma?" he interrupted her to ask.

"A coma is when a person goes to sleep and does not wake up for a long time, maybe never. It's when your brain is damaged and may not be able to be repaired. Anyway, when I did wake up I was here, so Jenny is back in my time lying in a hospital bed in a coma, while I am here to figure out how to help myself and my husband. Does any of this make sense?"

"I's unerstans' a litt'l, buts' I ain't sur' how's dis be possible'?"

"I don't have all the answers, but I am hoping that between the two of us we can figure them out, so I can get the ones I need to return to my life and my husband. I think I can also help Jenny with the Master Thomas problem, but I will need your patience and understanding to do so. Can you handle

89

what has been happening to your Jenny, concerning Master Thomas?"

"I's havin' a hard time of it, buts I's will tries. How yo' gonna bes able ta helps us anysway?' Jacob asked interested.

"If I can get to the bottom of why Master Thomas is the way he is, and what brought all the hatred of his own kind on, then I can help him see it as well. I think once he realizes his own problems and how he treats his slaves he will want to change and make things right. There is still a good man inside of Master Thomas, and I seen what that man is capable of, but I am not kidding myself about the tyrant that lives within him also. He hates what you and Jenny have and seems to want the same love that you two feel for each other, for himself; he just doesn't know how to get it." Tamaria finished knowing she was on to something big, but not sure if she could do all the things she was claiming the capabilities to do.

"Alrights', I's will helps ya, I's wants my Jenny frees' o' dat man an' I's wants ta bes happy as I's can be wit her. I's knowd' she cain't helps what da Massa dos' ta her, buts she won' sees it dat ways. I's undrestan' why things be so akward' wit us sometimes' now," he told Tamaria with hope in his eyes. "I jes hopes dat wes' able ta fix da Massa."

90

"Jacob I hope we can fix him too. I really do, because if not you may be stuck with me instead of your Jenny. I will not go back to my husband if I don't feel I can make a change, I can't, I'll be dead within a few months if I do. So lets pray to the good Lord above all goes well!"

The very next day when Jacob and Tamaria awoke to the sound of the plantation waking up they sat up in the little bed that was Jacob and Jenny's, and realized they had their work cut out for them. It was going to be a very long and hectic day, what with all the work required of them both, the selling of Jacob to contend with, and the puzzle that was Master Thomas, to be figured out. Each turned and began to dress for the days events without speaking; it was a very odd silence, one of complete understanding as to what was ahead of one another. Together they were forming a bond that few would understand, but it wasn't a bond of love or lust, it was a bond of two people desperately trying to save their lives. The situation was indeed dire, due to the circumstances surrounding both their loved ones. Tamaria needed to succeed with her tasks in order to have a happy and safe marriage to Darien, and Jacob must not fail or he would loose Jenny to a life and time he could barely comprehend. When it all came to the bare essentials, they were forced to be partners in an odd sort of dance with fate.

Chapter 8

Back on the Home Front

As Natillie sat staring at her sister's body in the hospital bed all thoughts, but one, left her head; she was furious with what had happened to her sister. She knew Tamaria had caused her own humiliation, by staying in her doomed marriage to Darien, but she still loved her sister. Natillie wanted her sister to finally get what she deserved; the best. Tamaria had always been a beautiful, vibrant, and likable girl, but the way their father had controlled them and shoved them in whatever direction he felt would benefit him had slowly destroyed Tamaria's vivacious spirit. Natillie still held her father responsible for all the heart aches her and Tamaria had endured in their lifetimes. Natillie had come out of it a winner, she had fought against the totalitarian she called her father, and ran away with her boyfriend at an early age. Life hadn't been easy, but the lessons she had learned while on the run from her own family had at least been her own

choosing. She hadn't stayed with the jerk she had run off with, because he had wanted her to abort the baby she had become accidentally pregnant with (as if using no protection at all was an accident); the only accident was the accident of stupidity she shared with the uncaring jerk for a brief time period. That situation really didn't matter anymore, because shortly after he had left her high and dry for not aborting she had lost the baby.

Natillie knew her experiences were a joyride compared to what Tamaria had endured living with their father. Tamaria was made to pay the price for what Natillie had done, she was never let to have freedom or to enjoy life's little pleasures. Their mother had died shortly after Natillie ran away from home, which left nothing as a buffer between Tamaria and their dad's hatred of women. Shortly into Tamaria's senior year of high school she had been introduced to Darien through their father, whose name was also Darien. He had been impressed by the accomplishments of the young Darien in the car sales industry, and saw their similar names as a sign from above that he should somehow connect this smart young man to his family. In reality their father had seen a lot of dollar signs if Darien was to marry into the family, and felt sure that Darien would be very giving to his new father-in-law. He couldn't have been more wrong. Once Tamaria was convinced that Darien was the only one for her, and decided to marry him, both Darien and their father had quickly put together a small wedding so that she didn't have time to change her mind. The quick engagement backfired on Tamaria and Natillie's father even quicker; because once Darien had gotten what he wanted he broke all ties with any of Tamaria's family members. Darien was an even bigger control freak than Tamaria's father had been, and meaner. For a short while, Tamaria was very content and happy with the break from her family, especially her father, because of all the claustrophobic feelings they had created in her over the years. Soon, however, that would change as Darien became more and more jealous of anyone or thing that took her attention from him. That was the beginning of the many years of abuse Tamaria had endured and was continuing to do so.

Natillie was so lost in the past and all the horrible events that had led to her sister's comatose state that she never heard the hospital room door open or the quiet footsteps that followed.

"Excuse me for interrupting your visit with your sister, but my name is Dr. Chasm Liteseeker and I was wondering if

95

you could answer some questions for me?" came a calm, but very strong womanly voice from behind her.

"Oh, please forgive me Dr. Liteseeker, you startled me a bit. I didn't hear you come in the room. Of course I will answer whatever you need to ask, or at least try to anyway," she said still a little off kilter from her trip into the past.

"Well, this may seem very odd to ask, but are you very close to Ms. Jackson's husband?"

"No, no ma'am I'm not. He is a very unusual individual and we have never quite hit it off. I'm sorry, but if your questions concern him; I'm probably not the best person to answer them," she replied with an undertone of anger in her voice. Natillie couldn't help it, she hated Darien and had difficulty masking that hate.

"I'm only asking, because I'm a bit confused about his recent behavior concerning your sister, so don't trouble yourself about it," Dr. Chasm left hanging out in the air for Natillie to grab hold of and reply.

"What behavior would that be? Darien was here, in this hospital? Did he try to hurt my sister, you had better tell me if he tried to hurt my sister Dr. Liteseeker, because I have a right to know," Natillie said as if she were a mother lion protecting her young.

"Calm down, Ms., I'm sorry I'm not familiar with your name?"

"It's Natillie, Natillie Brown ma'am. Excuse my anger, but I believe my sister's husband is the reason she is in this hospital bed, and I want to know what else he has tried to do."

"Actually your sister's husband, Darien I believe?"

"Yes, that would be him," Natillie replied impatiently.

"Yes, well at any rate Darien came to me with concerns that your sister may never come out of her coma. He was very adamant that he really did love his wife and was sorry any of this had occurred. I was at a bit of a disadvantage, because I wasn't sure what he was talking about?"

"He was concerned? That is a joke, one of the funniest I've ever heard," laughed Natillie sarcastically.

"No, I don't think you understand he has been here several times, and each time he has been furious that your sister is wasting his money and time remaining in this hospital in a coma. I have been ready to call security due to his crass and horrible behavior towards his wife, but the other day something was different about him."

"Yeah, he was hungry and didn't have any clean clothes to wear. He needed his little slave wife to come home and do all the work, and act as his punching bag when he got upset," Natillie spat.

"I'm serious, he was different, and so I lagged behind and watched through the glass window in the wall of this room to see what he would do. Do you know what I saw? I saw him yelling and screaming at your sister, and I was just about to call security to remove him once and for all when he collapsed in a heap at the side of her bed sobbing. He cried for a full hour. I kid you not; I stayed and watched. I was afraid he might still hurt her. Instead what I witnessed was a man in love and scared of loosing the only person in his life that mattered."

"I find that hard to believe, considering his past treatment of my sister," Natillie said in disbelief.

"I would normally agree with you, but I watched it all happen. He slowly stopped crying and began to talk to your sister. He would caress the back of her hands ever so lightly, as if she were about to break, then reach up and touch her cheek very tenderly while he kept talking to her. I wanted to know what he was telling her, so I snuck over to the door and pushed it open slightly. He never noticed, because he was so busy telling your sister how sorry he was, and that he'd do anything to change what he had done to her over the last couple of years. He also told her he missed her and to hurry back to him, because he had a lot of making up to do for all of the wrong he'd done to her. I was so touched listening to him, that I realized he really meant what he was saying."

"Well, I must admit, if he didn't know you were listening he had nothing to gain from saying all of that to Tamaria, but I still won't believe it till I see it Dr. Liteseeker. I've watched him and he never changes, no matter how many times he promises too," Natillie said as if she were too tired to listen to anymore of the nonsense.

"I understand how you feel, but he came and talked to me after he was through talking to your sister. He asked me what he could do to help her get better, he begged me for my help as a doctor."

"What did you tell him?" Natillie asked.

"I told him that if he really wanted to help his wife, he would seek therapy to help himself from destroying her. I handed him the card of a colleague of mine that dealt with physically abusive men. I thought I might get met by defiance, but he simply took the card, shook my hand, and said thank-you; then he left."

"Yeah, exactly like I said, he will never change! You can bet that card landed in the nearest trash can available!"

"Wait a minute, later that week I received a strange phone call from the colleague I had referred your brother-in-law to asking me to give him a call. When I finally did, he told me a Darien Jackson had asked him to call and thank me once again for him. I asked what that meant, and was informed that Darien had gone straight to my colleague's office after talking with me and made an appointment. I guess he is doing very well and improving with leaps and bounds. One of the things he has been told to do is to stay away from your sister until he knows he can control his anger. I haven't seen him in this hospital since. Instead of hurting her, he is trying to protect her from his issues and problems."

"Oh my God, I never thought I'd see the day! I hope he sticks with it. Will you keep me updated on his progress, we don't exactly talk?" Natillie asked Dr. Chasm.

"I don't usually share such confidential information, but in this case I will definitely keep you informed."

"Thank-you Dr., it means a lot to me. My sister is all I have in this world, and I don't want to loose her. I only wish Darien would have realized his feelings before this happened. Now, Tamaria may never come out of her coma."

The very next day as Natillie sat at her sister's bedside wishing she would sit up and start talking to her, she heard the hospital door open yet again. Thinking it was Dr. Liteseeker she turned around with a smile on her face, but it soon faded when she saw who it was; Darien.

Chapter 9
Master Thomas' Delight

Life had not been very eventful since Tamaria and Jacob had decided to work together to get her back to her own time. Master Thomas had left on a business trip the very same day that they had conspired to figure out what was the cause of his hatred, so nothing but work had been done. The daily drudgery of a house slave was wearing Tamaria down, she began to think she would be stuck in the past forever. She missed her house, bed, kitchen, and sister; but most of all she missed the ability to do what she wanted, when she wanted to do it. Everyday there were dishes to scrub, floors to clean, shelves to dust, utensils to polish, food to cook, water to be brought up to the big house, and so many other chores, that she could hardly stand when she finally left the kitchen to go home at night. Jacob was usually very quiet when she came into the little cabin, so there wasn't even good conversation awaiting her arrival. Since the very day she had told Jacob who she was he had begun to act differently around her. He had started to avoid her, even pretending sleep on occasion when she had returned home at night. Tamaria wished she had never confided in him, and had let their existence together remain emotional. Unfortunately she couldn't let that charade continue, but now she was all alone in a very strange place and time. She couldn't remember ever feeling so alone, not even when she had lived with her father after her mother had died and Natillie had ran away. All she could think about was Master Thomas and Darien. What was their connection, and how was she going to solve Thomas' issues with women and black people? The problem with it all was her not having the opportunity to try. If Master Thomas didn't get home from his business trip soon, the tree might come asking her to return home before she ever figured out what his problems were.

As if Tamaria's prayers were heard by God above the very next day Master Thomas arrived back at the plantation, but his mood was so fowl that all the house slaves were walking on eggshells when they were forced to be within the vicinity of him. He had walked in the front entrance screaming for his manservant to come and get his boots off before he placed them directly up his ass.

"Where the hell is everybody? Have all the slaves on this plantation up and ran away in my absence? If I do not have Adam in this very hallway in about two minutes, I will place my very large boot straight up his ass!" Master Thomas screamed.

He stood in the entry tapping his foot on the hard wood floor as he were a racehorse waiting to be let out of the starting gate; aggravation shown all over his face, and it seemed as if he were looking for a reason to punish someone to relieve his tension. Tamaria heard his yells of fury all the way into the kitchen, and began to feel a little hope surge through her. She wasn't looking forward to dealing with his anger, but at least he was home so she could try to get into his head. She quickly wiped her hands on a nearby dishcloth, and then turned to go and greet the master of the plantation. As she rounded the corner from the kitchen that lead to the hallway to the entranceway, she caught a glimpse of Adam on his knees before Master Thomas trying diligently to get his master's boots off without angering him further. However, that was impossible at the moment, because Thomas wanted nothing more than to pummel anything that came within a foot of him. He was so enraged at the dealings he had just been a part of, and the treatment he always received from any of the white businessmen in the area that he needed to vent his fury. He wasn't a black man any longer, at least not the type they were accustom to (slaves), but certainly wasn't white either. He felt like nothing had changed, he was still that unwanted little boy of the past that was trying so hard to be worthy of attention and praise.

Just as Tamaria was entering the foyer, she witnessed Master Thomas kick Adam so hard in the chest that he was thrown backwards and landed on his butt with a thump. "Idiot nigger, what is wrong with you? Can't you even manage to remove a boot from my foot? I should send you back to the fields you incompetent fool. Go away from me before I have the overseer whip your hide so hard you drip blood!" he screamed ferociously at Adam.

Adam scurried away in fear, as fast as his legs and arms would allow. Tamaria was so sickened by what she had just witnessed that she threw caution to the winds and came at Master Thomas with every intention of beating him till he bled.

"Well now, do you feel better? Hurting a defenseless innocent man must make you feel all warm inside. I'd bet that you wouldn't try that kind of nonsense with any of your fabulous white business friends, would you? What in the world has any of us done to make you hate us so much? Is it our color, because like it or not you share the same color skin as the rest of us; and you had better come to terms with it before you rot in hell for all eternity!" she yelled at him with conviction.

"Where the hell did you come from, and who the hell do you think you are speaking to me like that?" he said as he rose from the stool by the door. He came towards her with a menacing look that made her rethink her actions. She slowly began to back away from him, but she was so angry with what he had done to Adam that she continued to taunt him with her words, "I came from the kitchen, where all good little house slaves tend to spend their lives working their fingers to the bone to put food on the table for ungrateful Master's of plantations such as yourself! Oh, and I believe I am a human, which gives me every right in this world to tell you about yourself whenever your acting like an animal!" she replied in a much lower voice, but with the same conviction in her words. She stopped moving backwards and stood her ground. As Master Thomas came closer and got right in her face, she waited for the inevitable; she waited for the pain and degradation of being beaten by a man. To her great surprise, he began to laugh at her. Before she could react he

106

had grabbed a hold of her and pulled her against him to partake in a searing kiss. Master Thomas kissed her like he had missed every little piece of her. She felt herself go limp and then the deep burning began down at her feet; slowly rising into her body and through her private areas as well as her limbs. All she could think of was if he kept kissing her like this she would forget why she was so angry with him soon, and never be able to get to the bottom of why he was the way he was. In an instant Thomas let go of Tamaria, he just stood looking into her beautiful amber eyes as if he were a drowning man. The kiss he had given her made her feel as if she had just been burned, but the look he was now giving her almost had her turning tail and running for the nearest hiding place. This was what she needed to occur if she was ever going to get to the bottom of his soul and search around it, but the feelings he was evoking in her were to scary to contemplate. She wasn't sure she understood this extreme passionate feeling that came over her when he touched her in a sexual way. After all it wasn't as if he was professing his ever lasting love to her, he was simply showing her the lustful nature that came over him when he was near her. Thomas stood staring at her for a long time before he asked her a very peculiar question, "Did you miss me while I was away Jenny?"

Tamaria almost fell over, what was he talking about! "NO, I did not miss you, what type of game are you trying to play. I was very happy to be left alone with Jacob, so why would I miss such a mean individual as yourself," she replied with as much anger as she could muster after his searing kiss.

"Oh, you missed me alright, or you wouldn't have came running when you heard me enter the house?" he said with a devilish grin.

"I did not come running, and it wasn't because of you; it was because I heard some maniac throwing a temper tantrum and figured I'd better contend with them so nothing got ruined!" she replied matter-o-factly.

"Well why don't we just test my theory, and take this argument upstairs where I can receive a proper welcome home from you; or are you to frightened of how you'll react?" he teased her.

"I have no fear of how I will, would, or have reacted to your advances!" she yelled at him before she realized the quandary she had just gotten herself into. Oh dear God, now she would have to go upstairs and be alone with him. Tamaria tried hard to think of reasons that she could not accompany him to his rooms, and then she came up with one.

"However, I can not go with you at this time, because my chores are not finished. I guess a slaves work is never quite finished; is it Master Thomas!" she told him with great satisfaction, never expecting his reply.

"Oh but that is the great thing about being the Master of a plantation and not a slave, I can release you of your daily duties and assign them to another whenever I want! So let us see, ANNIE, ANNIE, could you please come here."

Tamaria was in a state of stunned silence. She had just entered into a place she had hoped to avoid; Master Thomas' sinful hell of a mind. It was true that she needed to delve into it soon, but was she ready to play his games yet? She took a deep breath and waited for Annie to come into the foyer.

"Yessa Massa Tom, what's yo' be needin'?" said Annie as she rounded the corner and entered the front of the house.

"Miss Jenny will be otherwise detained for a while today, so if you would please be sure that her duties are completed I would be very grateful. Is that alright with you Annie?"

"Yessa Massa, that be no problems at all. I's gets it all don' fo' yous' can blinks yo' eye," she replied.

109

"After you my dear Jenny, after all ladies first, that's what I've been told anyway."

"Yes sir, I suppose you would have to be told something like that!" she said under her breath as she moved towards the staircase.

"What was that I heard you say?" he asked as he laughed behind her.

"Nothing, I was just saying how I was looking forward to the challenge ahead of me," she replied sarcastically.

Thomas was giddy with the thought of being alone with Jenny again, he had not been able to get the last evening they had spent together out of his mind. Truth be told, Thomas had been so worried about what Jenny and Jacob were doing in his absence, that he hadn't been able to accomplish much of anything while he was gone. Finally, he was going to be able to settle this need he had inside, once he got her out of his system he would feel better.

Once they reached the Master Thomas' bedroom, Tamaria stopped and stared at the door as if she were doomed to die hanging from a noose. Thomas noticed her hesitation and began to think it was going to be another evening filled with her fighting him and him wanting to strangle her, but then before he could comment she reached out and turned the knob of the door and entered of her own accord. Maybe this wouldn't be such a bad evening after all, Thomas thought.

Tamaria glanced around the dimly lit room and immediately found her gaze landing on the giant four poster against the back wall. The memories of the last time she had been in this room came flooding over her, she could barely breathe. I can do this, she thought to herself, I can get inside of him and reach his inner person. Tamaria was trying to give herself a pep talk, but the nerves in her body weren't listening. She felt her body begin to shake and her blood seemed to drain right out of her in a large puddle at her feet. She knew she would find pleasure in bed with Thomas, but she couldn't get caught up in passion there had to be emotion as well, or this was never going to work. She decided she would come at him with everything she knew; she would bring on the big guns to fight this war of wills.

Tamaria turned as Thomas shut and locked the door behind them. He looked at her through passion filled eyes and she knew exactly what he wanted from her, but he wasn't getting it for free. He would have to pay a price that was very large; he would have to open up to her. She looked up at him and decided to go for the big prize; she would make him fall in love with her.

"I have missed you, Thomas. I hope you don't mind me calling you Thomas, but I think at this very moment Master Thomas doesn't quite fit. I have been thinking about you, and the wonderful passion we shared in this very bedroom. My mind and stomach did flip flops when I heard your voice, so of course I came running. I just didn't expect to see you being so mean to Adam," she said in a low seductive voice. Thomas almost stopped breathing, he couldn't believe his ears. Had Jenny just confessed to missing him while he was gone?

"What games are you playing here? Since when have you ever missed me, or looked forward to my return? I'm not as stupid as you might believe, so fess up, what are you trying?" he said as if he had just been burned by a very hot flame.

"I'm not playing any games with you; I really was looking forward to your return. Jacob and I have not been doing very well since he overheard what had been going on between us. I thought he loved me more than that, I thought he would be more understanding of what has been going on, but he just backed away from me. I don't want any man that doesn't want me! If you don't want me then tell me now, and I will leave," she baited him.

"I never said I didn't want you, so settle down. What exactly has been going on with you and Jacob?" he asked interested. "Nothing, he avoids me," she almost laughed when she said this, because Jacob avoided her only because she wasn't Jenny; but Thomas didn't know that. "And he acts like I'm not his woman anymore."

"So you two are finished with one another?"

"I still share his cabin, but things aren't good like they used to be."

"So, why are you being so lovely to me? I was the cause of all the distance that now exists between the two of you, why don't you hate me for ruining your one great love?" he asked slyly.

"Listen, you may not understand this, but you woke up something strange inside me the night we made love in this room. I know, I know, we have been in this room many times before, but never like the last night before you left. You were tender and kind, for most of the evening, and I got a glimpse of the man behind the monster." She told him seriously. Tamaria realized that what she was saying was what she was really feeling, and the rest just seemed to roll out of her like melted butter.

"I have to admit up until that point I hated you and every minute I was forced to spend with you in this room. That has changed now and I'm not sure I know the complete reason why. All I do know is that you and I have certain chemistry, and I'm ready to explore what that may mean for the two of us."

"I'm not sure I believe you, but I really don't care what your reasons are for co-operating in this bedroom with me. I am your owner and as such I will get what I want when I want it, if we understand one another then the so called "monster" that I can become shall lay dormant. Do we have a deal?" he asked.

"I know you believe you are superior, because you bought and paid for me, but I am going to show you what loving someone can make you feel. So as for a deal, I suppose we do have a type of agreement. I will continue digging into the chemistry that is between us when you're not a raving lunatic, and you will have a willing bed partner. However, I would like a little promise from you, are you willing to give it to me?" she cajoled.

"I am willing to hear you out," he said with a tiny smile of appreciation, "but I will not guarantee you anything until I've heard your proposal."

"For every night of passion and pleasure that I give to you freely, I would like one full hour of casual conversation between just you and I?" she said while watching the expression on his face.

Thomas wasn't sure what Jenny thought she was going to gain from talking to him, but it really didn't matter as long as he gained her body without a fight.

"Sure, I can do that. It seems simple enough, but what exactly are you looking for Jenny? It won't change anything between us, I won't free you or change my position on this plantation because we talk with one another," he said to her bluntly.

"It will allow me to get to know the man inside of the master, and you will be able to see the human inside of the slave. It is just a simple thing really, why should you care if I mean nothing more to you than a night of pleasure here and there?"

"You are quite right, dear Jenny, you are only a little piece of pleasure in an otherwise dreary existence, so it really doesn't matter to me what your reasons are."

"Then we have a deal?" she asked.

"Yes, we most certainly do!" he replied with excitement in his voice.

115

Thomas couldn't help but think how Jenny had just given him everything he ever demanded, and he wasn't giving up anything. He had won, or at least he thought he had. Tamaria, however, knew she was much smarter than he anticipated; she knew what to do to gain his trust and she was willing to do it.

Chapter 10

The Beginning of the End

It had been a full two weeks since Tamaria had made her deal with Master Thomas, and in that short span of time he had insisted she move her meager amount of clothes and possessions into the dressing room off of his bedroom. She had been required to sleep with him every single night of the two weeks. While Tamaria mulled over the beautiful nights she had spent with Thomas, she also contemplated the conversations they had after their lovemaking sessions. At first the conversation between them had been stilted, then as the days had gone on things had changed. She first noticed it just two days earlier, when Thomas had came rushing into the house in a foul mood from his business dealings with the town's politicians. He was furious. He stomped into his bedroom where Tamaria was supposed to be waiting for his return, and began telling her every detail of what had occurred; he never thought twice about what he was telling

117

her, he just talked to her like a husband would to his wife. She had listened patiently to all his complaints and problems, then asked him," What exactly do you want to do about this Thomas? The way I see it, they are blackmailing you, because you're a black slave owner. I know how frustrating it can be to be black and not seen as an intelligent human being, but what options do you have?"

He had stopped in his tracks and stared at her like she was a god send. "Oh my God, your right, what options do I have? They see me as a dumb nigger, and by God I should be taking advantage of there stupidity! Why didn't I see this before, if I refrain from selling them my cotton and tobacco they'll have to pay the higher price that the white plantation owners around here charge? I can go and meet with the other owners and make a deal with them to not sell to them, so they get their full price, but only if they sell my cotton as their own. I will get the price I deserve, make the other owners happy, and not have to pay their ridiculous fee for the privilege to sell in the city of Savannah!" he explained gleefully.

Thomas had then ran towards her, grabbed her up off of the settee she was resting on and kissed her on the forehead. He had thanked her for her help, and told her not to wait up for him that evening. He was going to be busy with business for the rest of the day and into the evening.

Tamaria was still in a state of shock. When he had come home he had snuggled next to her and promptly fell asleep. The next couple of days had been glorious between them, him sharing his plans for the plantation, asking her advice, making love with a passion that drowned out the up and coming decision she had to make when the tree decided to come for her, but today the reality had hit her and she was nervous. Tamaria had yet to hear the three words she was waiting for; I love you, Jenny. Thomas had been close the day he had discovered what to do about selling his cotton and tobacco, but he had still held back. Tamaria knew tonight she was going to have to push him a little harder than she had been doing; she was planning on asking him about his parents. Every time she had headed in that direction in the past he had changed the subject and become morose and moody. She hadn't pushed it for fear of ruining the fragile relationship they were building, but now she knew it was a subject that would never be broached without a shove from her. Before she could do that she had to get things settled with Jacob. She hadn't even thought of him over the last two weeks, she had been to involved with Thomas to pay attention to Jacob's feelings. She was concerned about what would happen when she left to go back home and Jenny returned. She walked down the stairs and into the kitchen area to find Annie; she had to talk to her about what to do about Jacob. She knew it appeared strange to all of the other kitchen slaves, now that she was sharing the master's bedroom and hadn't spoken to Jacob in weeks.

As Tamaria walked into the kitchen all talk ceased between the other slaves, they all looked at her as if she were their master too. She walked directly towards Annie and ignored their whispers behind her back. She knew they thought she had sold herself to the devil, but they had no concept about her dilemma. As Tamaria approached Annie she became nervous. She wasn't sure how she would be received now that she was considered Master Thomas' little whore, but to her delight Annie turned around when she heard approach, and when she saw it was Jenny she reached out to pull her into a huge hug.

"Oh dear Lawd', I's been so worrieds abouts ya Jenny! Is yo' alrights'? Has da massa hurts ya any?" Annie quickly questioned.

"No, no, I'm fine Annie. Master Thomas has been very kind to me, but that's not why I came to speak to you. I need to talk to you about Jacob," Tamaria said calmly.

"I' knew it was a cummin', I's told dat man o' yo's to thinks on what he was up ta, but he paid me no never mind," she softly exclaimed under her breath.

Tamaria noticed the other women paying close attention to her reaction to Annie's words, so she politely asked, "Annie, can we take a walk to the well and discuss this in private?"

"Oh, yes, yes hunny chile', we's most certainly cans," she replied understanding that Jenny didn't want to be the center of anymore gossip.

As they strolled down the dirt path towards the well, Tamaria couldn't help but remember when Jacob had come walking towards her while she was fetching water from the well on a day not so long ago. He had been so beautiful in the sunlight, how sad it was that he wouldn't even speak to her now. She hoped she had not ruined anything between him and Jenny, by pretending to be her before telling him who she really was. When they finally came upon the well, Annie walked over to it and seated herself on the rim so she could rest her feet for a spell. Tamaria decided to join her. Annie turned and stared into the deep hole dug into the ground where the well had been placed over, then she said something that caught Tamaria's attention, "Jenny, I's so sorry. I's cain't believes all dis has happened ta ya. I's don' knowed wahts ta say dat can makes it betta'."

"Annie, what are you talking about? I'm really confused," then Tamaria had a sinking thought that made her blood run cold, "Annie did Master Thomas sell Jacob off the plantation?"

"Oh dear Lawd's no, Jenny. Calms yo'sef. I's wish it was so's easy. Ya's really don' knowed what Jacob has done's, do ya's?" she asked with pity in her voice.

"No, I don't. Annie what has he done?"

"Jenny, Jacob be stayin' wit dat little strumpit dat works in da kitchens' wit usin'. He been goin' over ter her beds fo' da whole times da massa has kep ya up in dat room o' his. He done lef' ya hunny. He tolds me he don' wants notin' ta do wit a womans likes yo'sef. He thinks yo's enjoyin' wat da massa be doin' ta ya. I's tried ta explains ta Jacob how's ya had no choice an all, but he don' mades his mind up and lef'," she finished with tears in her eyes.

Tamaria understood now why Annie had been so concerned about her, and she was very upset by the news of Jacob. She

122

had thought he truly loved Jenny, but apparently he couldn't believe Tamaria's story, he simply didn't care.

"It's okay Annie, I haven't been home in two weeks and I haven't even talked to Jacob in the whole time I've been gone. I can understand why he did it; I'm just a little confused. I thought he really loved Jenny, I mean me. I guess I was wrong. Well I guess that makes my job of talking to him a little easier. I won't have to explain a thing, I'll just tell him I've fallen in love with Master Thomas and no longer want to be with him anyways," she stated.

"Yo's in luv's wit da massa? Jenny, oh hunny yo's better watch yo'sef, he be likes a snake, never knowed whens he goin' ta bites ya."

"I know, but he has changed Annie. I've been watching it, and I know there is a very good man somewhere inside of him. I hope I can help bring him out."

"I's jes' glad ya's ain't to upsets wit Jacob's leavin' ya's. I's was so scared of yo feelin's on it. I's hope ya can change da massa fo' good, but I's have my's doubts'."

"Annie do you know where I can find Jacob so that I can talk to him?"

"He be downs by da barn wit da hosess'. Jenny bes carefull, Jacob ain't been to happy's lately, Annie warned.

123

"Thank you Annie, I will." Tamaria said knowing she still dreaded the job ahead of her. She had broke Jenny and Jacob's relationship, and she felt horrible about it. Everything had been going so well, but now she wasn't sure what was going to happen. When Jenny returned and found Jacob had moved out and left her, what would she do? For that matter, how would she react to Thomas? After all it was Tamaria that had consigned herself to a peaceful existence with Thomas; Jenny was the one that fought tooth and nail to get away from him.

Tamaria walked down to the barn to find Jacob, and as she got closer she became furious with him for being disloyal to Jenny. How dare he treat her like a possession? He was no different than Master Thomas, and she intended on telling him so. She saw him before he saw her approach, and thought what a shame that he had to turn out to be a vindictive jerk; Jenny and he would have made some beautiful babies. "Jacob, can I speak with you?" she yelled across the barnyard.

He turned and saw her walking toward him; she could see fear cross his face. So the almighty Jacob was frightened of her was he, she would teach him a thing or two. "Jacob, come here right now, unless you want me to start yelling and screaming at you from over here; your choice?" she threatened.

He almost ran to get to her before she could embarrass him in front of the other slaves that were present. "What's yo' needs Jenny?' he asked with exasperation in his voice.

"I want you to be a decent loving man, but it's too late for that now isn't it Jacob," she said as he got closer. Then she walked up close to him, so that her body was pressed against his and he had to lean down to hear her words. Her breath was warm against his neck and she could feel him reacting in a very manly way.

"Jacob, tell me something, does little miss thing make your privates stand at attention like I do?" she whispered ever so softly in his ear.

"Jenny, what's yo' tryin' ta do's ta me?' he said breathlessly. "Make a very important point, dear Jacob! You are a waste of beautiful man flesh, and you just threw away the best thing you ever had; Jenny! I told you I wasn't her, but you didn't believe me, and now when she does come back she'll end up falling in love with Master Thomas just like I have. So why don't you go think on that while your all hot and bothered over me and screwing Eve!" she said between her teeth, then calmly turned and walked away leaving Jacob with his mouth hanging open; confused and lusting after her body.

Tamaria felt she had avenged Jenny's reputation and headed back to the big house to wait for Thomas.

Chapter 11

Battle of the Sexes

When Tamaria returned to the house she headed straight for the stairs and to Thomas' bedroom, but what she wasn't expecting was to find him there waiting for her. As she walked into the room she felt a chill roll over her shoulders and wondered if she was coming down with the flu, then out of the corner of her eye she spotted a person seated in the armchair by the large window that over looked the back of the plantation's grounds. Tamaria jumped from the fright of the surprise visitor, but on closer inspection she realized that it was only Thomas.

"Well I'll be you almost scared the color off of me Thomas. What are you doing home so soon?' she asked with relief.

"Really Jenny, now why is that? This is my room, and I do have the right to come here whenever I so choose. As for why I'm here at an unusual time well I was coming to tell you how well the plan for the sale of the cotton and tobacco had gone, but to my great dismay you weren't available for me to talk to. Why is that?" he asked with his teeth clenched so hard she could see the veins in his jaw pulse with blood.

"I had some business to attend to myself Thomas, nothing out of the ordinary," Tamaria replied vaguely.

"You are a slave. What business do you have, or could you possibly have to attend to unless I give it to you?" he yelled as he got up and came towards her.

"That is none of your business, and like it or not I won't tell you!" she yelled back.

Tamaria was so furious with him she almost turned and ran from the room, but common sense told her that he would just send another slave to catch her if she did. She slowly took a few steps toward Thomas with the intent of confronting him about his attitude towards her, but he put his hand up to stop her.

"Stay where you are, little Miss Rebel. You have a lesson to learn and I'm going to have to be the one to teach it to you. Get all of your clothes off now, and don't make me wait to long!" he told her in a low and menacing tone.

"I most certainly will not. I did nothing wrong; you're being an idiot. I had to talk to someone and tie up a few loose ends, that's all that happened."

"Were those loose ends to do with Jacob?" Thomas asked as he watched the shocked look come over Jenny's face. "Did you think I would never find out that you were lying to me? Am I that easy to fool? I must be stupid; I'll give you that, because I was actually starting to trust you!" Thomas finished as he turned from her and ran his fingers across his forehead. "I haven't lied to you Thomas; you can trust me. I did go to speak with Jacob, but..."

Tamaria never got to finish her explanation, because Thomas interjected with, "I can trust you alright, I can trust you to be screwing Jacob behind my back, and act like you only want me!"

Tamaria wasn't sure what to do; Thomas was past listening to anything she had to say. She turned to gain her bearings, and then realized she had to talk to him about his family life; she had to get him to see he was wrong about her. She knew he distrusted everyone, sometimes even himself, but she also knew that stemmed from somewhere in his youth.

"Thomas where were you born?" she threw at him. Thomas slowly turned and looked at her as if she were possessed. "What in God's name does that have to do with anything?" he asked.

"I want to know where you are from, what kind of people you come from, and what would make you so distrustful of everything and everyone around you!" She had finally voiced her needs; she hoped that he would hear what she had to say.

"Where I come from is not your business, but for your information I was born in Alabama in a town called Montgomery, where my family were slaves for a plantation named "Little Heaven." Does that make any sense to you? No, I didn't think it would! You can't always tell a book by its cover, now can you Jenny?" he spat at her.

"I certainly hope you can't, because if that were the case I'd read yours as a book never to be read."

"You think you know me? You think you can even begin to understand me, or the way I feel? Let me fill you in on the "real" Master Thomas. I was born on a plantation named "Little Heaven" where I grew to the ripe old age of fifteen. At that time my "Master" decided to mess up my family's whole existence by gambling away a good portion of what he had owned. The good news was that he could trade the man he was indebted to his slaves in place of the properties he had lost. However, being the type of master good ol' Master William Salient was, he chose to let each of the ten slave families choose one member of their family that would be traded off. He couldn't stomach what he had done and felt he had no right to choose for them. You see Master William had always treated his slaves like real humans; he had taught us to be families and promised not to sell our family members away to other plantations. He was a good "Christian" man, or so he claimed, so he did not believe in breaking up families. When the time came for him to give over the ten slaves he had promised to the creditor, my family chose me to be the one to be sold. Oh my mother tried to reason with me, she tried to make me understand that because I was the oldest child I was more capable of surviving such a drastic change. She kept crying and saying the children need your daddy and me, they're so young still. Then of course my father would tell me I was a man now and needed to act like such. At first I was stunned, then I realized what my own parents were doing; they were getting rid of me. I was no longer important and the least loved, therefore the most expendable. So you say whatever you'd like about me and my "own" people Jenny, but I know just what kind of people I came from and I don't trust the lot of you," he finally finished as if his heart had been torn out of him.

"Oh my God, Thomas I'm so sorry. I had no idea anything so horrible had happened to you when you were a boy. I'm..."

"Don't hand me your pity Jenny, I don't need it. I have not only survived everything my family threw onto my shoulders, but I came out the better for it. The man I was sold to took to me for some reason, from the very moment I jumped off the buckboard he looked at me like one of his own. I never did figure him out, but he gave me an education, he willed his land to me, he even introduced me to several people that have helped me survive as a free black plantation owner. That one white man gave me more in the matter of five years, than any of my black family had even tried to in fifteen. Unfortunately, Master Sam died when I had just turned twenty, so I've been on my own to run this plantation ever since. If not for him I'd have been sold down the river to another plantation, and probably another after they were through with me. You see Jenny, I don't hate only black people or white people, I hate all people. It's really very logical don't you think? There is one type of people I hate more than any other's though, and that is all thanks to my most loving mother; I abhor women. I have only one use for them, and most of the time their not even good at that," Master Thomas said to her with a challenge for her to try and prove him wrong. Tamaria could hear his pain and wanted to go to him and hug him close, she wanted to make him see that his mother had loved him; she had simply been left with an impossible decision to make. Tamaria slowly walked over to Thomas and reached out to touch him, he jerked as if he had been burned when her hands met his face, but he didn't pull away from her. She tilted his head up towards her face and leaned in to place a tiny little kiss on his beautifully pouting lips, then she very quietly and calmly tried to explain, "Thomas you most certainly do not hate women. You have been hurt by them, or one in particular, but it is not in the way you believe it to be. I listen to you talk, and I hear the emotion behind your words. Your mother tried so desperately to explain her reasons for choosing you instead of any other, because she did love you and felt she was dying inside from doing what she had to do. Thomas, she simply had no other logical choice, her children were all so young, and she knew they needed a father and mother; you were the closest she had that was close to being an adult. Your mother probably thought and worried about you every day after you left that plantation. I would bet that if she is still living, she is still dying inside over you and her great loss as a mother. If I were her I would have died the very day you walked out of my life." As he looked up at her with tears in his eyes, she leaned in and pulled him close to her. Tamaria hugged him and kissed him in a way she had never, in her entire life, done to any human being. She now understood the hatred and anger that were always right under his surface. She now knew why he had pushed Jenny to want him, even though she was in love with another. Thomas needed a woman to love him more than anything else in the world; he just had no idea how to get that without force.

Thomas was pulling her towards the bed; before she realized it she was lifted up into his strong embrace and placed gently on the mattress. He slowly removed his clothing while he stood next to the bed, the entire time staring at her with some emotion she wasn't quite sure of pouring out of his eyes. When he finally crawled into the bed with her, he simply looked at her and said, "I need you Jenny, I don't know why, but I know I need whatever you give me when we are together."
Tamaria melted at the sound of those words. She was lost. Her heart had been given to a scared little boy that needed love.

Tamaria woke with a start, where was Thomas? She had fallen asleep in his arms after hours of sweet love with him, and now it was barely dawn and he was no where to be found in their room. She hoped he had not woke this morning with regrets for having told her all of his childhood sadness. She was beginning to understand his horrible attitude towards his slaves and her. Thomas had been abandoned and felt worthless, so he tried to hide that emotion by keeping control over every tiny aspect of his home life and relationships. He did not seem to see the force behind what his mother and father had done to him; he was blinded by hurt. Tamaria wanted to help him to see the hopelessness that his parents had to have gone through, but she wasn't sure how she would be able to do that. She knew this was the key to unwrapping what was going on with Darien back in her future, and she was damn sure going to try to help Thomas past his problems; in doing so she just might solve her own.

Chapter 12

The Day After the Storm

Natillie was beginning to think there was no hope for her sister's recovery. Day after day she came to sit with, and read to her. Sometimes she just stared at Tamaria trying to will her to open up her eyes and speak, but Tamaria never moved so much as a muscle. Natillie had learned to avoid the rare visits that Darien would grace her sister with, she didn't care what Dr. Liteseeker thought about his so called changes; she knew he was always going to be a demon from the dregs of hell. She continued to listen to the updates that Dr. Liteseeker would occasionally fill her in on, concerning Darien's therapy, but ultimately she held no faith in him truly being cured of whatever mental disease he possessed. What it all came down to was Natillie only had concern for Tamaria, and she wasn't wasting any of her time on Darien. She missed her sister, she wanted to be able to talk and laugh with her again, and every time she thought of what that bastard of a husband

136

of Tamaria's had done to eliminate that possibility; the hatred grew.

Once again Natillie found herself lost in thoughts of revenge on her brother-in-law, and this is why she didn't hear the door slowly open to let the subject of her thoughts enter her sister's room.

"Natillie, it is so good to see you. You can't possibly know what it has meant to me knowing you were here to watch over Tamaria when I was unable to," he said startling Natillie out of her thoughts.

"Well, your feelings have not been my concern, my sister and her comatose state however, have been," she replied to his greeting rudely.

"Natillie I know you hate me and wish it were me in that bed instead of your sister, but what you don't know is how much I also feel that exact same way," Darien tried to reason with her.

"What in the Hell would even point to such a ridiculous thing? The fact that you have been beating my sister up on a regular basis for the entirety of your marriage to her, or is the fact that you didn't even want the hospital to keep her here due to the large amounts of money coming out of your pockets? Oh, or was it the fact that you left her for dead in the house you share with her, as if she were nothing more than your dirty laundry on the floor? You tell me why I should believe you have even the tiniest bit of remorse for what you have done to my sister, because I can't seem to find any reasons to believe you," she ground out with so much emotion that tears shone in her eyes and her chin quivered. "I swear to you I'm trying to get better. I have a disease of sorts…" he tried to explain, but Natillie wasn't through with him.

"You can go to every therapist there is in the entire state of Georgia, and you will still be the asshole that tried to kill my sister in my eyes! So save your crap for Tamaria, because I don't trust you; hopefully she won't when she wakes up either. Then what will poor little Darien do? Who will you abuse then? If my sister has any sense at all, she will run with her head on fire screaming "take me away from the bad man", to get away from you when she comes to. I just hope you spend the rest of your life suffering for the loss of her," Natillie yelled over her shoulder as she stormed out of the hospital room.

Darien walked slowly over to the chair next to Tamaria's bed and fell into it like a man defeated. He knew there wasn't anything that Natillie had said that he didn't deserve. He was so sick of feeling horrible; he wanted to find peace within his own mind. His therapist was very pleased with his progress, and up until his run in with Natillie, he had been, too. Now he was ready to give up, if he couldn't get Tamaria's sister to even listen to him; how would get Tamaria to forgive him and trust him not to hurt her again. Darien felt hopeless. He sat staring at Tamaria wondering how he gotten so far off the beaten path, and how he was going to get back on it without his wife. If Tamaria left him he knew he would finally let her go, he couldn't force her to stay with him using fear tactics anymore. He needed her trust to help him get past all the horrible things that had created him in the image he had become; he needed her unconditional love.

As Darien sat and thought about his current problems, he found himself remembering back to his childhood; with all of its horrors. He had only been five when his mother had first tried to get rid of him; she had left him with another woman that was selling herself on the streets of Savannah. When the woman had searched and found his mother a week later, she was so high and drunk that she didn't recognize her own son. The whore had left him with his mother anyways telling him, "Sorry hunny, I gots to do my job. I cain't be lookin' after a kid," and then hurried out of the scummy hole his mother was living in. He had been on his own for as long as he could remember. Darien had finally been left with his grandmother at the ripe old age of eleven, but by that time he was already ruined. He had watched his mother get beat up by her tricks, have sex with anybody that would have her, and been sold to several male tricks that had other interests other than what his mother could offer. He was so angry and lost when his grandma took over his care, that it didn't matter how good she was to him; he was determined to destroy himself. So he began racking up a police record from stealing, getting into fights, doing drugs, and possessing weapons that were illegal. His grandmother stood by him through it all, and tried to get him help; Darien would have none of it.

One day while spending some time in the juvenile delinquent home, he ran into a counselor that seemed to be interested in helping him. At first Darien wouldn't give the guy the time of day, he thought he was some kind of pervert who liked boys, so he blew him off. Jack Sanlin was an unusual man, and kept trying with Darien. It didn't matter what Darien said or did, he would still talk to him and try to be his friend. After Darien left the home he figured he wouldn't have to worry about Jack getting in his face anymore, but the day after he had left his grandmother received a phone call from Jack asking if he could be Darien's Big Brother. It took Jack months to break some of the armor away from Darien, but at last during Darien's junior year in high school Jack said something that woke him from his stupor.

"Darien, how long is going to take to break you of the mold your mother set you into? Are you trying to be a carbon copy of her? Do you want to end up on the streets eating out of dumpsters and selling yourself to get money for drugs, or better yet go to prison and become some big dudes bitch? Or would you like to make something of yourself?"

After hearing those words, Darien decided he wanted to do something with his life. He wanted to get rich and be powerful. He never wanted to be reliant on any other human, for the rest of his life. Darien had taken the help that Jack had been offering all along, he got hooked up with a self made business owner and millionaire, where he was given a job at a car dealership cleaning cars and trucks. It hadn't taken him very long to show the boss how smart he was and get moved up in the ranks to a salesmen, but Darien wasn't happy staying in that position; he wanted more. He went to the boss and convinced him to help him take classes at the local college for business. Before he knew it he was graduating with a Bachelors of Business Management with a 4.0, and the boss was putting him in charge of the entire operation. He still sold cars, but he was the General Manager, too. Darien was making money hand over fist, but he was missing something. He was missing a beautiful woman to parade around on his arm. That was about the time Tamaria's father had showed up on the car lot with her, he was looking for a used vehicle. Darien had wanted Tamaria from the moment he had seen her walking quietly behind her father with her head held down. Her hair had been cut to frame her face, and when she had looked up at him while he talked to her father; Darien had almost passed out from the beauty that shone out of her eyes. He had been drawn to her and shortly realized with a little charm he would probably be able to con her father into setting up a date for him. He had noticed right off the bat that Tamaria's father treated her like his property, and not a daughter. He had seen the gleam in his eyes when the offer of some money getting knocked off the price of a car was given in trade for a date with his daughter. Darien had watched how Tamaria behaved towards her father and realized she was the type of girl who wouldn't kiss and tell. She would do what she was told and that was exactly what Darien was looking for, so he proceeded to wine and dine her father and Tamaria; until the day finally came that her father agreed to them getting married. Once the ring was on her finger Darien no longer put up facades. He quickly rid himself of her family and began to isolate her from other people; he didn't want to take any chances of her getting around other men or somehow finding out where he truly came from.

For the first few months married life for Darien and Tamaria had been pure heaven. She had not minded his removal of her father from their lives; in fact she was overjoyed to get rid of him. She had accepted his wants for her complete attention, because she liked feeling needed and loved, and she had been more than amicable about any decisions that were made concerning where they lived and how they lived. She was the perfect woman for him. They would lie in bed on the weekends making love for hours, then go into the kitchen and cook up fabulous food to eat. Tamaria was such a good cook; he loved all of her inventions in the kitchen. Then one day he had come home from work to find her gone, he couldn't believe it. He had left her without a car or money. He was convinced she was out with another man and he had been being duped all the while. When Tamaria had walked through the front door whistling and carrying a bag of groceries she never expected what he was about to do, he grabbed her and began beating her. He had hurt her pretty bad that first time, but he had apologized and they had driven to a clinic to get her patched up. That was the beginning of all the anger and pain Darien had been feeling all his life getting released through abusing his wife for her so called misdemeanors. It got so bad that she would cringe when he went to caress her and make love. Instead of trying to help himself, he had gotten angrier and blamed her for the problem.

Now Darien was paying the price for all of the sins he had committed against his beautiful wife, and the problem was he couldn't even talk to her or try to explain why. He was a beaten man; he was utterly alone in a world filled with people who hated him. How would he prove that he was changing and becoming better for it?

Chapter 13

Time Flies When the Future is Waiting

Tamaria hoped that Thomas would return to the plantation soon. When she had come down stairs a couple of mornings past, she had been told that Master Thomas had urgent business to attend to and would return as soon as possible. She was sure that her time was about up, and she needed to see him one more time before she returned to the future. She knew she had to convince him to leave Jenny be. She had to get him to understand that if he simply acted like the good person that hid inside of his body, Jenny would fall in love with him. After all, Tamaria had fallen for him. He had given her hope that she and Darien might actually have a chance at a new beginning. He had shown her why a man would allow themselves to wallow in anger and pain, but he had also given her insight into the heart of a self destructive man. Tamaria had the feeling she would be going back home within the week; there was a sense of anticipation hanging in

145

the air. She would miss the quiet serenity of the country life on the plantation and she would miss Annie, but she wouldn't miss the lumpy beds, horrible work, and being owned by another human being. Tamaria longed to tell Natillie about everything she had learned. Natillie probably wouldn't believe her, but she was going to tell her anyways. She realized she was beginning to look forward to her departure, and smiled; it wasn't so long ago that Tamaria would have been grateful if she never had to return to her own home. Now she couldn't wait to walk through the doorway. No more would she back down from her husband and no more would she remain a prisoner of her own house. She was going to go back to college and get her education then she was going to get a job, and if her and Darien worked things out good enough she would start a family with him. Tamaria knew she was finally ready to face her future, but before she could do that she must deal with her past.

Thomas couldn't wait to show Jenny the surprise he had on the seat next to him in the carriage. He had been driving across the country for what seemed like forever, but it was actually only five days. After spilling all of his private business to Jenny he had made love to her for hours, and then as she lay in his arms sleeping he realized how relaxed he felt. It was the first time since he was a boy that he had felt so comfortable, and he knew what had caused it; the love of a good woman. Jenny was in love with him and he knew it. She might not know it yet, but he had his whole life ahead of him to wait till she was comfortable enough to tell him. He had thought and thought on what she had said about his parents, and finally he realized what he had to do; he had to find out if they were still alive and if they were mourning their loss of a son.

When Thomas reached the plantation called "Little Heaven" he felt his heart pop up into his throat, what if they were dead. What would he do if he couldn't find his parents? His thoughts surrounded the possibility of his parents having been sold to another plantation, but he couldn't bare the contemplation. Thomas was determined to think positively, so he drove up the long drive and hopped out of his carriage. The doorman gave Thomas a glare; he couldn't believe that a Blackman had the audacity to pull up to the front entrance of the house.

"Where yous' tinks yo be goin'? Massa don' lets no niggers in da front. Yous' goin'ta have ta go round da backs ta da slaves do'," he said as if Thomas must be mad to try anything else.

Thomas had just ignored him and walked right into the house. After all hell had broke loose, and William Salient had been disturbed enough to poke his head out of his study, Thomas finally told them who he was. Master William had been thrilled to see Thomas, and was willing to do anything to get rid of his guilt over having broken apart so many families. When Thomas said he was there to buy his parents freedom, William was more than ready to deal with him. Before Thomas knew it he was happily reunited with the parents he had spent most of his life hating. They had used the time it took to travel back to Thomas' plantation to fill each other in on what had occurred during their separation. Thomas was so happy, his mother had not been the same since he was sold off and his father had become lethargic and sick for a long while after, but since his return to their lives they had become almost youthful in their happiness. His siblings had either been sold to pay debts or had died. His mother told him of a terrible sickness that had passed through their area and killed two of his little brothers. His two sisters and other brother were sold off and would have to be tracked down. Besides the deaths of his brothers and selling of the other siblings, he was overjoyed at having his parents with him. He knew Jenny was going to be thrilled to meet them.

Tamaria heard Thomas calling for Jenny from outside the house. What in the world was he up to; he was finally home, and standing outside screaming her name for all to hear. She ran to the front door and pulled it open to find Thomas standing there with two people that appeared to be worn and tired. They were old and wrinkled, but happiness beamed from their eyes.

"Jenny, this is my mother Sally, and my father James. They are going to be living here on the plantation with us from now on. I bought their freedom from Master William," Thomas spilled out in a rush.

Tamaria almost passed out. She couldn't believe it, Thomas had listened to her; he had trusted her. Without thinking she ran over to him and began to kiss him all over his face. She couldn't help it; he had made her so happy. He was coming to terms with his childhood. There was hope for Darien after all.

"Oh Thomas, this is the best thing you have ever done. I'm so proud of you," she said to him then turned to his parents and said, "Sally and James I would like to tell you what a fine son you have here. He is a true gentleman." Tamaria felt like she was floating for the rest of the day. Thomas spent the day getting his parents rooms ready for them and introducing them to his slaves. He was so busy that Tamaria had no time to pull him aside and have a talk with him about Jenny. It wasn't going to be easy, but she knew she had no choice. Everything was going so well, she didn't want to pop Thomas' bubble.

Chapter 14
The Tree's Patient

The third day after Thomas had returned with his parents Tamaria finally found some time to talk to him. She had to get this over with, the tree was coming and she knew it. The evening before she had gotten up in the middle of the night feeling very strange and woozy; everything had seemed to shimmer in front of her. The whole bedroom was spinning, and she had felt like she wasn't even human. Tamaria had tried to walk towards the windows that lead to the upstairs veranda, but her feet felt so heavy she couldn't seem to lift them up. When Tamaria had glanced over at Thomas he had appeared to be a mirage; she had thought the tree was taking her back at that very moment. Tamaria had begged, in her head, for the tree to give her a couple more days to tie up loose ends, and suddenly she was able to move her feet. She knew she had been granted a short reprieve, but it was only a few days before there would be no more reprieves. Tamaria had to get this over with or she would leave Jenny in a fine predicament; not to mention Thomas.

As Tamaria entered Thomas' study, she glanced around at the beautiful setting he had created for himself. The bookshelves were crafted from rich, dark mahogany that gleamed, when the sunlight from the huge bay window lanced across them. There were hundreds of leather bound books on the shelves, which gave the room a manly aura. She took in a deep breath of air and realized it smelled like Thomas; spicy, dark, with a woodsy background. Tamaria would miss this old, but gorgeous house. Across the room sat Thomas in his big, brown leather, winged back chair. When he noticed her entering, a huge grin came over his face; it was a look of pure joy. Tamaria would also miss Thomas. Who would have ever thought that in such a short span of time she would grow so fond of this man. The changes in him were immense since first they had met, and all of them for the good.

"Well, well, well, to what do I owe the honor of such a beautiful woman's attention, so early in the morning?" he asked Tamaria in a light hearted fashion.

"You my dear sir, left this morning without saying good morning! So I decided to give you a second chance!" she joked back.

"My goodness, your right, how very obtuse of me. Come over here and let me see if I can make it up to you," he leered.

Tamaria knew what he intended, and she was very willing to go along with his sweet morning games; however time was short she was going to have to get to her point before things got out of hand. She knew Thomas wanted her; truthfully, she wanted him just as bad.

"How exactly do you plan on trying?" she asked as she slowly sauntered over to him.

Thomas reached across his desk and pulled her around to him; placing her on his lap, while wrapping his arms around her in an embrace that left her breathless. She couldn't help herself, she leaned into him and let him kiss her. She was swimming in the passion he was creating all around them, when she suddenly felt herself go numb. The room was spinning again, dear God, the tree was back again. Tamaria knew she had to stop this love play and get to her business. As she gently pushed him back in the chair, he gave her a confused, questioning look. "What's wrong Jenny?" he asked.

"Nothing is wrong Thomas, actually everything is very right, but I need to talk to you before we get too carried away with this moment and I forget."

"What could be more important than this," he said as he leaned in and nibbled on her neck.

"Thomas, please, your making me feel dizzy! I really do need to talk to you, can we take a few minutes, just a few, before I let you ravish me for the rest of this wonderful morning?" she asked with a cute little pout of her lips. She knew he couldn't resist the thought of making love all morning long, with the sun shining through the windows, and the entire staff of soon-to-be freed slaves' right outside their door. It was just to risqué for him not to love the idea.

"Alright, when you put it that way, how can I say no?" he laughed. Thomas adjusted himself in the seat, so he could pay better attention to what Jenny had to say.

"What is so important Jenny?" he asked casually.

"Thomas, how do you feel about me?" she asked back.

"Jenny, you know how I feel, if this is all that you wanted to know I can reassure you; I love you," he stated with no hesitation. The statement almost knocked the wind out of

Tamaria's sails. She was ready to throw the tree to the dogs and get back to making love to Thomas, but she knew that wouldn't solve anything.

"Thomas, would you wait for me? Would you give me time to adjust to all the changes in you? Do you love me enough to do that?" she spit out quickly.

"What are you trying to tell me Jenny?' Thomas asked as he began to sit up straighter and back away from her.

"I'm trying to ask how much you love me, what my love for you is worth to you, and how far you'd go to make sure that love was completely returned, without force," she finally got out.

"Jenny, are you telling me you don't love me? Oh please, tell me your not. Don't do this, I've just found some happiness, don't rip it away," he exclaimed in terror.

"No, that's not what I'm saying," she said as she watched the relief flood over Thomas. "I do have strong feelings for you, but they have been born under the watchful eye of slavery. I want to know that I feel this for you without having to, because I'm your slave. I need to be able to remove myself from you, just for a little while, and let you be who you are now. Then I will know for sure whether our feelings are true," she said with deep emotion.

"Jenny, I know I have forced you to be with me in the past, but that has changed. Can't you see the difference in me? I don't love you, because you're my slave; I love you because you freed me from my slavery to abuse. I was enslaved to abusing everyone and everything I came in contact with; until you. I know it has moved fast, but that doesn't mean it isn't true," he tried to convince her. Tamaria believed him, but when Jenny came back in her place; she would still feel the same way about Thomas as when she had been ripped away. She had to give Jenny time enough to realize the changes in Thomas, and to be able to fall in love with him. It was going to be shock enough for her to find Jacob moved out and with another woman, Jenny didn't need to have Thomas thinking she was his, too. Thomas had to understand, how could she make him understand, she needed to before the tree came back.

"Thomas, do you love me enough to let me adjust to all the changes that have taken place?" she asked as seriously as she could. She had to make him realize how important this was to her.

Thomas pushed her up off of his lap, and began to pace the study floor. He turned to her with tears in his eyes and said, "I love you so much my chest hurts when I look at you.

When you are lying next to me at night fast asleep, I pull you close and watch the emotions from your dreams cross your face; I watch your angelic expressions and weep with the joy of loving you. I wait all day just to be able to talk to you again. I can't eat, work, or sleep without you on my mind every second, of every minute of the day. I love you more than I love my own life, is that enough love for you?" he quietly whispered to her. "I love you so much that I would do anything you asked of me including breaking my own heart." Tamaria could bare it no longer, his pain was to great. As she ran to console him and tell him she was sorry, her dress caught on the corner of the desk and she tripped. She felt herself falling, but only heard Thomas' scream of panic as her head hit the wooden stand holding the world globe. She felt a numbing sensation leaking through her body, and then Thomas was at her side. She felt like she was still falling, because he seemed to be going further and further away form her. It was then that she realized that it wasn't the fall that was making her feel this way, it was the tree. She struggled to touch him one last time, as the tears streamed down his face, but couldn't move to do so; she had made her decision. She pulled all the energy she had left together and whispered vaguely, "I will always love you Thomas," then slipped off into the vortex of the tree.

Thomas sat next to Tamaria, his Jenny, and cried like a small boy. He thought she was dead. He thought he had lost the only woman that had ever loved him unconditionally. He was so distraught, that he didn't notice the slight movement from Jenny's body. He reached down and pulled her body into his arms; hugging her to him as if she were going to disintegrate. Suddenly he felt her stir, he thought it was his imagination, but then it happened again. Thomas placed her gently back on the floor, and watched her slowly come to. "Dear Lord, Jenny, I thought you were dead," he cried. "Master Thomas, why are you crying? Where am I?" Jenny said in confusion.

"You're in my study. You fell and hit your head; I thought I would die without you. Jenny, did you mean what you said?" he asked her hopefully.

"What are you talking about, how did I get here? What did I say?" Jenny asked him.

"You came in here to say good morning, and to make love to me in the sunlight. We had an argument, then you fell, but before you passed out you said you would always love me," he told her.

"Master Thomas, I don't remember any of that. I don't remember much of anything, but I do remember who you are, and who I am. I'm your slave aren't I?" she asked bewildered.

Thomas realized that when Jenny had hit her head she had lost most of her memories. What was he going to do now; would she remember him forcing her to be with him? Would she remember any of the old him? Maybe her memory loss was a good thing, maybe this would help him. Thomas knew he was back at the beginning with Jenny, but at least it was a good beginning; he loved her enough to wait for her to catch up to his feelings for her.

Chapter 15

Darien's Second Chance

Tamaria was floating in a whirlwind of memories. She could see herself as a child at her mother's funeral crying silently, then she was getting locked in her room by her father as a teenager, and then there was her marriage to Darien; memories just kept popping up before her, it was like watching a movie of her own life's events. Tamaria wondered where Thomas was, and if he was alright. She wasn't sure where the tree was taking her, but she knew it was far away from him. She was never going to see him again. Before she knew it she seemed to have landed on something soft. She was afraid to open her eyes, she wasn't sure if she was ready to face Darien or her sister. Would she still be in the hospital? Maybe Darien had gotten sick of waiting for her to wake up and put her in one of those old age homes. Oh please God, let me be in the hospital she thought to herself. Tamaria didn't think she could handle some crotchety nurse coming in and trying to make her use one of those terrible bedpans. She wanted to lay in the exact spot she landed until she was returned to the past with Thomas; she had never guessed how badly she would regret her decision to return to her present. She knew she still carried a hope for her marriage to be able to get better, but she had worked so hard at getting through to Thomas; now she would never know if she had truly succeeded.

Suddenly, Tamaria heard some steps and a door being opened, and then she felt the shadow of someone standing over her. She wondered if she should get it over with and open her eyes; letting the whole world know she was back from her journey into her own mind. Something stopped her from opening her eyes; it was the sound of Darien's voice as he knelt next to her bed and began to cry. She couldn't believe what she was hearing, Darien was crying; she had never known him to cry in the entirety of their marriage. She decided to wait and see what he would tell her comatose body, maybe it would help her to gain a little advantage over what she was coming back to. She felt Darien reach toward her; it took everything she had left in her not to jump away from his touch, but she managed. Darien looked down at Tamaria and a deep sadness welled up inside of his chest, he couldn't look at her without huge buckets of guilt washing over him; what was he going to do if she never recovered. The weight of his own emotions brought him to his knees, he needed to purge himself of this horror, or he knew he would never get better; he knew the beatings would continue with Tamaria or someone else if she never recovered. "Tam, I'm so sorry. I know I always say that to you, but I really mean it this time. I have never had to live without you in my life. Since the day we got married I have been counting on never having to be without you, but I'll be damned if I haven't taken you away from myself. All of my anger, hate, and meanness have been directed towards you, but it wasn't you I was angry with; it was me. I'm not worth the dirt on your shoes and I've always known that, I was so lucky to find you. You have been so good to me; you take care of me every day of my life. It is your face I go to sleep with in my dreams and wake up to in the morning. I think of you every minute of the day Tamaria, I swear I do! I'm always worried you'll finally see how much of a waste I am and leave me, so instead of giving you the chance I keep you scared and frightened of ever going against my wishes. I was once a good little boy, I swear I was; then my mother left and I lost all faith in life. Dear God, I've ruined everything, everything!" he sobbed into her hand. Tamaria could feel the wetness of his tears as they rolled down his face and onto her arm; he was a lonely little boy just like Thomas. She finally knew how to deal with Darien that was why she had been sent back in time; Thomas had been there to show her what to do to save her husband and marriage. She felt something welling up inside her heart for Darien that had been missing for awhile; it was love. God had granted her a chance to heal this man and in the process gain her own freedom from degradation and pain; how would she ever repay that merciful kindness.

Darien was still kneeling beside Tamaria when he began to feel a hand stroking his head, comforting him in his grief and pain. He thought the good Dr. Liteseeker had come into the room without him hearing her, so he glanced behind him, but no one was there. Suddenly he realized that Tamaria was the only other person in the room, he raised his head slowly to see if he had finally lost his mind; Tamaria's beautiful doe like eyes stared back at him. Darien let out a yelp of shock and began to back away from Tamaria as multiple thoughts crossed his mind, was she frightened of him, was she going to turn him into the police, thank God in heaven above his Tamaria was back. Tamaria reached out to him and gestured for him to come closer, so Darien began to walk back to her bed. He was going to do everything he knew how to get help and make his marriage a good one; he believed God was finally on his side. "Oh Baby, oh sweetie, I've been waiting for you to come out of your coma for so long. I'm so sorry...," but Darien didn't get a chance to finish his plea for her forgiveness because Tamaria interrupted him. "Darien, I heard everything you said a few minutes ago, you don't have to talk anymore; just listen to what I have to say, okay?" she questioned. Darien just stood next to her nodding his head in agreement; the only thing he could think was that she had heard his confession and grief and what she would think of him now. "I experienced many strange emotions while I was unconscious, and it brought me to some conclusions about us; our marriage is a farce. It is built on needy people trying to find each other in a dark cave filled with anger and pain; I don't want to live in that type of marriage anymore." Tamaria watched as Darien's face fell and he began to speak, "Tamaria I love you, no matter the past, I love you, and I will do whatever you think is best for you. I may not have been the best husband or friend to you throughout our marriage, but I want to change that; I want to make you proud of me. I'm sorry for the pain I've caused you and will never be able to change what I've done in the past, but the future can be a

warm and loving place and I plan on making sure it will be."
Before Darien could continue Tamaria interrupted again,
"Darien, do you think I'm planning on leaving you?" Darien
looked at her in puzzlement and said, "Yes, isn't that what
you're trying to tell me?"
"No, I'm telling you that I am a very different woman than
what I was before the coma. I'm stronger and more capable
of standing up for myself. I won't be beaten down by you or
anyone else in this life ever again. I love you Darien, but I
don't trust you; yet. I want to try a separation, but only for
the time it will take for you to get healed from all the
childhood issues your carrying around in that heart of yours. I
plan on being there through it all and holding your hand to
lead you through the rough spots, but until I know you're
through the bad spots I want to ensure my safety. Can you
deal with that?" she asked him quietly. Darien couldn't
believe his ears; Tamaria was willing to give him another
chance. "Tamaria I feel like I need to remind you of who you
are speaking to, I'm a bad seed and I'm not totally sure I will
be able to get better. You deserve better than me." he stated
dejectedly. Tamaria stared into his eyes and saw a little spark
of what she had witnessed in Thomas when he had finally
figured out why he was so angry at the world; it was then that

she knew everything would be alright; eventually. "Darien you are not a bad man, but you have done some bad things. We can get you past it; I have faith in the inner being that was once a good boy. Are you ready to walk down the path to happiness with me?" Tamaria said with a smile. At that moment Darien realized he was the luckiest man in the universe, he had Tamaria and he had a chance at a better life. As he leaned in to hug his long missed wife he whispered in her ear, "If you can forgive me, I will spend the rest of my life trying to make your life the best it can be. I love you Tamaria, and there will never be another for me." Tamaria felt tears well up in her eyes as her husband began to kiss her ever so tenderly. Her thoughts began to swirl and she decided he had better heal quickly; she wasn't sure how long she would be able keep herself out of their marriage bed.

Epilogue

All Bad Things Must Come to an End

Tamaria raised her head to the sun filled sky with joy. Life was good. She needed to get back to her sister's before Darien arrived to take her out to dinner, but she wasn't worried, she knew he would wait patiently. She could barely believe what her life had become, she had a job at a school watching little kids on a playground and she was enrolled in Culinary School as well. She would never have guessed this would ever happen for her, but in the two years since she had been in a coma and visited her past, her life had improved daily. As she hopped in her car and began to drive towards her sister's house she thought of some of the bumps her and Darien had had to overcome. Her sister Natillie had been very unforgiving of Darien, it wasn't until recently that she had finally let go of the past and began to give Darien a chance; now they seemed to be enjoying each others company and even talking on the phone when Tamaria wasn't home. Darien had been going through therapy for the entire two years and it had been nothing but improvement after improvement for him. There were mild set backs when Tamaria had started to work and go to school, but he had gotten through it and realized she wasn't going away from him. Darien had finally gotten to the point he was supportive of her endeavors. The best part of all was that she felt safe when she was with him; that was something she had never thought she would feel again.

Tamaria turned down the road and saw Darien's car in her sister's drive, butterflies began to flutter in her stomach. Tonight she was going to tell Darien a little known secret, and she was a little nervous about it. As she pulled in she saw Darien step down from her sister's doorway and begin to walk towards her, she couldn't help but feel proud of her man; he was so gorgeous. Natillie followed him out and down the drive to her, a little grin played on her face because she was the only other person that knew Tamaria'a secret. As Tamaria got out of her car she was embraced in a giant bear hug from Darien, "Damn, you get more beautiful by the minute. I missed you." he stated simply. Tamaria laughed and shook her head at him, "If I didn't know better I'd think you had did something wrong, spewing all those compliments!"

Natillie walked up next to them and asked, "Where are you two off to this evening?" Tamaria answered slyly, "Anywhere that they serve huge amounts of good food, because I'm starved!"

Darien played along with them, "You better watch it now, or I'll be married to the prettiest chubby girl anyone has ever seen!" he joked. Tamaria looked at her sister and winked, "Oh is that what their calling pregnant woman now a days?" Natillie just stared at Darien waiting to see his reaction, but he was just laughing at the joke with them. All of a sudden he stopped abruptly and turned to Tamaria his face ashen in color, "Did you say pregnant woman? Aaare yyyoouu pregnant?" he finally got out. "Why yes dear, I am. What do you say I move back in to our house and we raise us a nice little family?" Darien let out a sudden whoop of joy and grabbed Tamaria around her waist to twirl her in the air with him, "A baby, a baby, oh wow, a baby!" he kept repeating over and over again. Natillie looked at the two people that were her family and finally felt relief that her sister was safe and Darien was going to be good to her, "Well Darien I hope your vocabulary improves before the baby is born or it will have a very limited education from its father!" she said with a giggle! Darien reached over and cuffed her jokingly in the shoulder and then grabbed her in his wife's and his embrace, too. They all stood there together knowing that this was the beginning to a very happy family.